THE STARLIGHT WISH

Janice Bennett

Zebra Books
Kensington Publishing Corp.

http://www.zebrabooks.com

ZEBRA BOOKS are published by

Kensington Publishing Corp.
850 Third Avenue
New York, NY 10022

Zebra and the Z logo Reg. U.S. Pat. & TM Off.

First Printing: November, 1999
10 9 8 7 6 5 4 3 2 1

Printed in the United States of America

For Terrel

Prologue

The lyre hovered in midair, just above the herb-strewn kitchen table, playing a lively melody on itself. Morning light streamed through the lace-hung window and sent iridescent rainbows off the crystalline notes that floated visibly about the sweet-smelling room. Eighth and sixteenth notes, chords and glissades swirled and spiraled in a dance to their own music.

A woman of medium height stood at the table sorting sprigs of thyme and rosemary, humming softly in time to the lyre, sending an occasional grace note skipping merrily amongst its fellows. The thick plaits of her long blond hair looped about her head, with stray strands falling to brush the shoulders of the long blue tunic she'd knotted about her plump waist with a silver cord. As one set of her double oval wings beat slightly in time, a single round feather, transparent except for its golden tip, drifted to the floor. Xanthe loved music. Over the countless ages she had dwelt in this tiny cottage and garden, she had gathered a remarkable collection of instruments.

She had also gathered a cat—unless, of course, it had been he who had gathered her. The enormous white feline now lay in a patch of sunlight amidst the herbs that covered the massive oak table. Sprigs of aromatic basil and oregano clung to his long white fur, but he paid them no heed. A rumbling sigh escaped him as he stretched to his full length, then rolled on his back, his considerable expanse of stomach exposed to the warm rays.

The fairy's hum changed fractionally, and the bundle of thyme she had just fastened floated to the rafters, where it hung itself on a peg to dry. Resuming the original tune, Xanthe turned to the window, where her rush basket lay overflowing with lavender and rose petals. She reached for its curved handle, but a sudden glint from the sideboard caught her attention, and she turned to the chased silver basin that rested on a lace runner there.

The mirrored interior reflected a star-filled midnight sky, in staunch defiance of the decidedly sunny late morning. The surface rippled, sending sparks of colored light fracturing, glinting about the room like a crazed kaleidoscope. From within its shallow depths, the water began to roil, sending bubbles and wavelets splashing against the gleaming sides.

Xanthe's eyebrows rose, and her violet eyes, full of mischief, lit with pleasure as she peered into the turbulent waters. "Titus, you're neglecting your job," she informed the cat.

The tip of the feline's thick tail flicked, his ears twitched several times; then his sleepy green eyes opened. Tiny stars reflected in his pupils.

"It's about time you woke up," she declared.

Titus responded with a sleepy sound, which was not quite a meow. That would have cost too much effort.

"That's no excuse," she informed the animal. "Come lend a hand and let's see what this is."

The waters stilled, but the prismatic lights continued their erratic dance, sparkling about the room, colliding and entangling with the forgotten notes that hung suspended in midair, awaiting her further direction. Xanthe dismissed them with a wave of her hand and a hummed measure. She needed to concentrate on the images that began to take hazy shape in the interior of the mirrored basin.

Stars flickered into existence, wavered, then vanished behind thick storm clouds. Darkness engulfed the waters. Then another star peeked out, brilliantly blue, tinged with vibrating hues of yellow, green, violet, and pink. An unseen wind blew cumulus clouds across it, but the single star glowed through.

Titus rose, stretched, transferred his considerable bulk to the sideboard with the lightest of leaps, and peered inside. He emitted a series of short, staccato sounds.

The waters swirled within the basin and the clouds vanished, leaving only that solitary sparkling light.

Xanthe hummed softly, yet the surface of the waters remained turbulent. "Starlight," she murmured, and opened the drawer directly beneath the bowl. She rummaged through the contents: an array of candles in a variety of colors; quartz crystals of differing sizes and shapes; innumerable stones; herb-stuffed sachets woven of a spider's fiber on her tiny loom. At last, from near the back where it had lain hidden beneath a crescent fashioned from her own rounded wing feathers, she drew forth a crystal star. A soft exclamation of satisfaction escaped her as she held it up to the bright rays of the morning sun and watched her treasure shimmer.

Titus settled on his haunches, wrapped his luxuriant tail about his feet, then licked a front paw and used it to tidy his whiskers.

Xanthe cast him a reproachful glance. "I can't tell yet."

She sent the five-pointed piece of delicate crystal to hover above the bowl, then searched through the drawer once more until she located a blown-glass box through which she could see half a dozen iridescent tapers. These she set in star-shaped glass holders about the bowl. She hummed three notes, and the candles burst into flame. Titus's low, rumbling purr began deep in his throat as he added his mite to her workings. They waited.

For a moment, nothing happened. Then the six tiny lights reflected off the hovering crystal star and back into the basin and the shallow waters. The kaleidoscope of brilliant particles danced off the rippling surface, then stilled as the waters turned milky white. Light shone from within, as if they burned with their own fire. Then the water cleared, opening a window into another world.

Titus leaned forward, and his nose twitched. He

emitted a sound that might have been taken for *prrrt* by the uninitiated.

"A man," Xanthe agreed as the image of a face appeared, as plain as if the gentleman stood on the opposite side of a pane of glass. Strong features, more rugged than handsome, dominated by a nose of classical proportions, wide-set hazel eyes, and a chin that bespoke stubbornness. Tightly curling blond hair, cropped short in a military style, topped his high forehead and a face more accustomed to giving orders than accepting either help or suggestions, more accustomed to frowns than laughter.

Xanthe drew a deep breath, reaching across the distance between them, attuning herself to this oddly stern fairy godchild of hers. At once, she felt the weight of the responsibilities that lay heavy on his broad shoulders, felt the determination, the rigidity. "He won't bend easily," she mused.

Titus fixed her with a stare of feline intensity.

"Major Aubrey Kellands, now the fifth earl of Daventry," Xanthe informed her companion. "And, yes, I believe he's going to prove every bit as difficult as he looks."

Titus blinked and leaned closer to the bowl.

"He has much to learn," Xanthe agreed, "and I fear he's going to resist us every step of the way. Which means," she added as mischievous laugher lit her violet eyes, "we are going to have fun. What was that?" She glanced in suspicion at the cat as the tip of his luxurious white tail twitched. "Well, of course. He'll be having fun, too." Her cheek dimpled. "Though he might not realize it at first."

She hummed another few notes and passed her hand over the basin. The water rippled, and the image reflected in it wavered, then faded. She continued to gaze into the mirrored depths until stillness returned once more. A sigh escaped her and she stood, stretching, her wings expanding, then settling once more along her back. A gold-tipped feather drifted lazily to the ground.

Xanthe looked to the cat, who stared back, the picture of feline indifference. "Don't give me that. You're as eager to go back to work as I am. How soon can you be ready to leave?"

Titus opened his mouth in a silent meow.

"Excellent." Humming softly, she pointed a finger at each candle in turn. Each promptly puffed out, then danced its way back into the glass box. Xanthe liked to leave things tidy.

One

It didn't feel as if he were coming home. He knew the turns in the road, of course, and many a time in what now seemed the distant past he had stopped for ale at the White Hart Inn, which they had passed not half an hour since. But though the thatched roofs of the village cottages, the ancient smithy, even the ruins of a tumbled wall were all as familiar as the great rambling house he had escaped eleven years ago, he felt separated from them, as if they were naught but pictures he had viewed in a book long since put back on the shelf.

Major Aubrey Kellands, the fifth earl of Daventry for a scant four months, hunched his shoulders against the drizzling rain. It had begun about five miles back, pouring down in torrents at first, as if the heavens sought to rid themselves of every last drop. His rangy chestnut gelding, as seasoned a campaigner as he himself, paid it little heed, merely laying his ears back and thrusting out his Roman nose in belligerent defiance.

His companion, the cousin who had shared his regiment until the action at Borodino had cost him his right arm, shifted uneasily in his saddle. "Not the best possible homecoming weather for you, is it, Aubrey?"

"We've known worse, haven't we, Clumsy?" Daventry patted his horse's streaming neck, then gazed ahead through the bleak cold of the mid-December afternoon. "Lord, remember the mud your horse sank into on that damned Portuguese plain?"

That brought a fleeting smile to Captain Frederick Grayson's tightly set mouth. "I remember that ravine better. I thought we'd never get everyone through."

Daventry cast a covert glance at his cousin. Frederick's customary inconsequential joking had slowed with the onslaught of rain, and the past hour had passed mostly in silence. The sooner they got themselves within doors, the better. His hands, cold despite their serviceable gloves, eased on the reins, encouraging his mount to a trot.

Frederick caught up to him. "You'll find the Court much changed."

Daventry's jaw set. This was the first mention either of them had made of his ancestral home, that great, rambling pile his father had let go to ruin. He'd managed to thrust most thoughts of it from his mind during the years of his soldiering, but he could do so no longer. So many bad memories haunted him, interspersed with a few good ones.

Anticipation stirred within him. He hadn't seen his half sisters since the youngest was in leading strings. Sophronia would be fourteen now, and Arabella seventeen. Young ladies unseen, but thankfully not unknown. His father had forbidden him to communicate with them, but with Frederick's help he had smuggled them little presents and notes, and they had reciprocated.

At the top of a rise he reined in, gazing across the wide, shallow valley toward the manor house that stood on the low hill across from him. The peaks of the towers protruded above the tops of the trees, just visible in the indifferent light. He spurred Clumsy forward, down the sloping grade, beneath the tall pines that cast their dark shadows over the muddy cart track.

Another quarter of an hour brought them to a road leading to the left. They followed this for a distance, at last coming in sight of a gate that stood ajar, hanging from a broken hinge. A stray beam of sunlight illumined the rusted wrought iron; the misting rain had let up at last, allowing patches of blue sky to peek out from between the dense clouds.

Frederick gave vent to an exaggerated sigh. "Now it turns fair. I might have guessed."

"Of course you might." But Daventry had few thoughts to spare for the weather. Only a quarter mile more along the gravel drive, then around the bend . . . and there it stood, Kellands Court, that low, rambling Elizabethan manor onto which generations of Kellands had added wings and towers and archways. Numerous chimneys sprouted from the rooftop, mullioned windows filled every wall, and ivy, rampant and lush, wound its way everywhere.

He studied the facade, and the general air of dilapidation and neglect appalled him. The gloomy weather added no spark of cheer to the place, and

nothing could disguise that no one had trimmed the
hedges nor tended the paths. Had it really been
eleven years?

They turned through the archway of the stable,
where he was pleased to note some semblance of
order held sway. Within moments a small, wiry figure stuck his grizzled head out of the low building,
then gave a shout over his shoulder as he threw
aside the pitchfork he held. Two more grooms,
younger lads, followed him into the walled yard.

The first man cast a considering glance over the
two riders. "Captain." He nodded to Frederick; then
his frowning scrutiny fell on Daventry. "M'lord?"

Frederick leaned forward, balancing himself with
care as he kicked one foot from the stirrup and
swung to the ground. The little man was beside him
in a moment, catching the reins, allowing Frederick
to straighten his coat with his one hand. "This is
Hewlett, your head groom, Aubrey."

"I'd have recognized him anywhere." Daventry
dismounted. "It's been a long time, Hewlett."

The little man grinned. "That it 'as, m'lord. And
good it is to see you again. Welcome 'ome. 'Ere,
you take 'is lordship's prad, and be quick about it,"
he called to one of his minions.

After seeing Clumsy and Frederick's mount led
away to their quarters, Daventry turned with his
cousin and crossed the dying lawn, the weed-studded
gravel drive, then climbed the shallow steps to the
front door. For a moment he stood there, mustering
his forces, then applied the knocker.

"Not at your own home." Frederick, grinning,

thrust the door wide and strode into the hall, shouting for Finley.

Daventry followed in his wake, both eager and loath to be back.

Only things weren't as he remembered them. Furniture had been shifted to different positions, knick-knacks removed, and everywhere lay a fine film of dust. That had never been tolerated in his stepmother's day. He looked about with a sense of disgust, noting the faded hangings, the dull tarnish that clouded every metal surface, the hint of mildew in the air. It revolted his military sense of cleanliness and order.

Footsteps approached quickly from the back hall, and the next moment an elderly majordomo materialized. He stopped short, staring from one to the other of the new arrivals, and a broad, welcoming smile spread across his narrow features. "Master Aubrey—your lordship, I should say." He came forward with a surprisingly rapid step. "Such a surprise! And on such an afternoon—" He cast a reproachful look at Frederick. "If you had but sent us word—"

"No matter," Daventry assured him. "It's good to see you again, Finley. Do you go on well?"

"Very well, thank you, m'lord." He eased the dripping greatcoat from Daventry's shoulders. "We had no idea you would be here today, or we should have had all in readiness for you. But there's a fire in the Blue Salon." He divested Frederick of his coat, as well. "If you will go in, I will see to some refreshment." With that, he bustled down the hall.

From somewhere above, a young female voice called, "Cousin Frederick? Is that you? Have you brought him?" Then: "Sir? Are—are you Aubrey?"

"Of course he is," hissed another voice. "Who else would it be, silly? He looks the very image of Pappa."

Daventry's heart lurched. He moved to the foot of the stairs and gazed up at the two wholly unfamiliar young ladies who stood in the gallery above, leaning over the railing. Both wore sadly rumpled merino gowns quite out of fashion and streaked with dust. His half sisters. The younger—it didn't seem possible she could be little Sophronia—held a begrimed rag in one hand.

"We aren't ready for you yet," Sophie cried.

Such an air of accusation colored her voice that for the first time in hours, Daventry grinned. "I beg your pardon. Shall I go back out into the rain and wait?"

"Sophie, your manners!" cried the elder. "Whatever will he think of you?"

"That you are both still the abominable little brats I left behind," came his prompt response.

Arabella burst out laughing, her constraint vanishing. "Odious beast!" she cried, falling back on the childhood epithet. "I, at least, am a grown lady now."

"Indeed you are. You have both grown out of all knowledge since last I had the pleasure of seeing you."

It bemused him to see them so grown. Eleven years—eleven very long years—since the death of their mother removed the last buffer between himself and his father. He shook off the painful memory and regarded his half sisters. "What are you doing cleaning?"

Arabella descended the stairs with all the awkwardness of a damsel determined to display a grace her seventeen years lacked. "Just keeping ourselves busy until you arrived. You can have no notion how long a wait it has seemed."

Sophie bounced down after her sister, eyeing Daventry with a critical, measuring frown. "You're taller than Pappa," she announced when she stood before him.

"And you're as pretty as your mamma. Both of you." He spoke no less than the truth. Both had that lady's rich brown hair with its glowing mahogany highlights, though unless memory failed him utterly, Arabella's shone a shade darker. They also possessed remarkable fine eyes fringed with thick dark lashes, Sophie's more blue, Bella's more gray. They boasted no more than average height, Bella tending toward a pretty plumpness like her mamma, Sophie more wiry and solid like her father.

"Where is your aunt?" he demanded abruptly.

The girls exchanged an uneasy look. "She left us," declared Sophie with an air of unconcern.

"Left?" Daventry glanced at Frederick, who appeared as startled by this bald statement as he. "Do you mean you are here alone? With no female to look after you?"

Bella spoke a shade too quickly. "There is Mrs. Whitlaw."

"Mrs. Whitlaw." That would be the housekeeper. He remembered her name from those tedious talks with the solicitor who had administered his father's estate. She didn't appear to excel at the housewifely virtues.

He cast an annoyed glance about the shabbiness of the entry hall, which in his memory gleamed from waxing and oiling, the sunlight sparkling through the lace hangings, flowers spilling out of their bowls on every table. . . . He fought back the sense of loss. If only his stepmother had lived, he might never have left the Court, in spite of his father. "What the dev—deuce did your aunt mean by leaving you to the servants? When did she go?"

"Two—" Bella began.

"Almost three weeks ago, now," Sophie corrected her elder sister.

Bella shot her a warning glance. "Well, it is of no great account. She was quite doddering with age, you must know. She found her duties here taxing, so she begged her younger sister—our Aunt Tabitha—to come and take her into her household."

"Leaving you alone?" Daventry repeated.

"Well, as to that, it was no great matter," Bella declared a touch too airily. "We assured her we would be quite all right, because you would be arriving any day."

He studied her guileless face, and didn't fall for it for a moment. "What brought matters to a head?"

Bella cast Sophie a warning glance, to which her younger sister paid no heed. "Bella wanted to be brought out during the Little Season."

Bella sniffed. "Well, why should I not? I turned seventeen. And I quite thought she would enjoy the treat, but no sooner did I bring it up than she took to her bed and declared herself incapable of enduring the rigors of a Season."

"She had us fetch Dr. Horley," Sophie added. "And when he assured her there was not a thing wrong with her, she announced seeing him brought on her palpitations, and nothing would do but she must seek the peace of her sister's household, and wrote to her at once."

"I see." He studied the girls, the one defiant, the other quite cheerful, as if driving away their chaperon were of no matter. He cast a sideways glance at Frederick. "It seems I have left my return a little late."

"Much too late," agreed Bella with gratifying promptness. "We have done our best to keep the household running," she added with a dubious look about.

"I see." Daventry kept his tone even. "And why does Mrs. Whitlaw not see to it? Where are the maids?"

Finley returned at a stately pace down the hall, bearing a tray laden with a variety of biscuits and cakes, interrupting any answer. A footman followed, carrying a pitcher, a teapot, two tankards, and a selection of cups. These they bore into the Blue Salon, and Daventry ushered his cousin and sisters after them.

Here, too, the general air of neglect struck him. The room wasn't exactly shabby, but it had a faded appearance. It lacked the brightness and cheerfulness that had permeated the entire house when his stepmother had been there. He fought back the memory of the sweet woman, as silly as she had been pretty. He had learned to love that flighty creature in place of the mother he had never known.

The servants proceeded to lay out a vast array of refreshments on the table. Daventry regarded it with consternation. "I thought we were to dine shortly. Do you not still keep country hours?"

Finley inclined his head. "Normally, my lord. But I have had the meal put back half an hour to allow you time to change."

Daventry met his cousin's look of comical dismay. "I fear our baggage is somewhere on the road behind us."

Sophie selected a sweet biscuit. "Then we shall all dine in our dirt. We shan't mind in the least."

"What I won't mind," declared Frederick, "is sampling some of these. I'm ravenous." He gathered freely from the abundance.

Daventry shook his head. "You won't want your dinner."

"Oh, won't I just." Frederick grinned at him. "Here, try some of these. They're devilish good." He passed a plate heaped with hearty cakes filled with nuts and dried fruit.

Daventry waved it aside and turned back to Finley, who had retreated to the door. "Would you send Mrs. Whitlaw to me?"

The majordomo hesitated, his expression prim with disapproval. "She is feeling poorly, my lord."

"She is always feeling poorly." Sophie selected another biscuit.

"She took to her bed shortly after Aunt departed." Bella's gaze drifted to the cakes, then hurriedly away. "We've tried to keep things going," she added, with the expression of one who knows the effort has not been sufficient.

"Has a doctor been summoned?" Daventry demanded.

"He was unable to find the cause of the problem," Finley informed him.

"I see." Daventry frowned. He had a strong suspicion the malady could be described as terminal laziness.

"We have been preparing a room for you," Bella offered.

"Pappa's," Sophie added. "It is not quite perfectly ready, but if we can get Alice to make up the bed, you should be quite comfortable."

"Alice? Then you do have a maid?" He couldn't keep the dryness from his voice.

"We have two," Sophie said proudly. "Aunt insisted we hire another after Pappa died, and we did not think you would mind."

"You should have hired a dozen," came Daventry's prompt response.

The sound of crunching gravel reached them, and he strode to the window in time to see an ancient baggage coach pull up before the house. A moment later his batman jumped down, followed by Frederick's valet. The two men set about unloading a variety of trunks and valises. Finley went at once to see to the arrangements, and Daventry followed him into the hall.

"You." He signaled a footman, who hurried from the back of the house to go to his superior's aid.

The young man, lean and angular, came to a respectful attention. "Robert, if you please, m'lord."

"Robert," Daventry repeated, "would you send the maids to me? The captain will be needing a room prepared, and this hall is somewhat in need of a dusting."

Bella emerged from the Blue Salon. "We had meant to see to it before you got here." She eyed him with wide, apologetic eyes.

"At least dinner should be to your liking." Sophie, with three biscuits in her hand, joined her sister. "Pappa kept a first-rate cook."

On that promising note, he allowed the two girls to escort him up the stairs to the chamber he would occupy. He knew the way perfectly well, but he found it easier to enter in the company of his half sisters. If it weren't for the fact that the earls of Daventry had always occupied this apartment, he would have preferred to ask for his old room, that small chamber one floor up and in the next wing which he had used from the time he had left the nursery suite until he had found continued residence beneath the same roof as his irascible father impossible.

"Do you like it?" Bella's worried words broke across his troubled reminiscences.

He looked about, frowning. No trace of his father remained. In fact, only a few pieces of furniture stood about the room. No bedding, no decorations, only unfamiliar faded burgundy hangings. His battered trunk lay in the middle of the floor. "You've been busy," he stated. "And to good effect."

Sophie beamed at him. "We are not quite done, of course. If you think you would prefer another room for tonight . . ." She let the sentence trail off and regarded him with a dubious frown.

"This will do me very well. Did I never write to you about the peasant huts we slept in on one campaign, with their dirt floors and a hole in the ceiling to allow the smoke to escape and the rain and mosquitoes to come in?"

Sophie brightened. "This is positively a palace in comparison."

"Indeed it is." He held out a hand to each of them. Sophie grasped one at once, Bella after only a moment's hesitation. "Thank you. Shall we leave the task of setting all to rights to my batman? I assure you, he knows from long experience exactly what I like."

With that, the girls agreed, and with no little relief. Smiling, he sent them to their rooms to tidy themselves for dinner, then turned to face the emptiness of the apartment. At least nothing remained to remind him of the many reasons he had left. Perhaps living here would not be so very bad after all.

The door opened behind him, and Kirk, his batman, staggered in beneath the weight of a well-packed valise. This he set on a chair, and at once set about unpacking sufficient clothing for the earl to dress for dinner. After half an hour of enduring the man's outraged silence over the disordered state of the apartments they were to inhabit, he escaped downstairs garbed in clean, if not impeccably pressed, garments suitable for a gentleman dining quietly in the country.

The Blue Salon stood empty. Apparently he had readied himself faster than the others. He poured himself a glass of Madeira from the decanter on a pier table, then went to stand before the hearth, surveying the room.

Tomorrow he would have a lengthy meeting with the estate agent, then make a list of everything that needed to be done. It would take time for the farms and houses to recover from so many years of neglect, but at least he had sufficient funds to lavish where they would do the most good. His father's man of affairs in the City had made the situation abundantly clear. His father had spent almost nothing except for his own comfort over the eleven years since his second wife had died.

It would take more than money, though, to make the house a home again.

Which brought him to the problem of his two half sisters. Arabella was quite right; she ought to be presented during the coming Season. He would have to find someone proper to chaperon her, show her how to go on. Then there was Sophie. She needed a governess, he supposed. Lord, had either of the chits any accomplishments? They'd never discussed such matters in their infrequent letters to each other. He should probably engage instructresses in music, modern languages. He'd have to discover what was considered de rigueur.

He paced the length of the room, fighting back the sensation of being overwhelmed. He was a soldier, had been with the army since the age of seventeen. He knew nothing of managing a family. If he were still in the army—well, why not consider it that way? If he were a commanding officer, faced with a situation where he didn't know how to proceed, he'd find an expert—a woman, presumably one who knew both household management and the social world into which his sisters were crying to be admitted. He ran his relations through his mind, but his memory of them was hazy at best.

What he really needed, he supposed, was a wife.

He strolled to the window and stared out into the darkness. The rain had stopped completely, but thick clouds still veiled the sky. As he studied the bleak December night, the clouds separated, revealing a single star. If he had one wish, the thought drifted through his mind, it would be for a wife—a capable, managing wife of suitable birth and upbringing. The estate needed a lady of the manor. He needed one, too. Then he could hand these mysterious matters into her efficient hands, freeing himself to deal with the neglected lands.

He ought to marry anyway. He was nine-and-twenty, past time he should be setting up his nursery. His only heir was a distant cousin he had never met.

Restless, he let himself out of the salon and paced across the entry hall. A wife. An eminently practical solution. But where was he to find one? He didn't want to return to London until he had matters in hand here—but in order to get those matters well in hand, he needed the help of a wife. He opened a door at random and realized he had entered the library. The old twinge of guilty enjoyment struck him, for his father had forbidden him this room with its convenient egress toward the stable yard. But his father was dead.

He fetched a taper from the hall and lit the first candle he encountered, then the others in the silver branch. He had always longed to explore this room. He started forward, then halted abruptly.

Before him, sparkling lights glittered in the air. As he watched, they took on a vaguely human form, then exploded. He blinked as luminous peacock feathers cascaded to the Aubusson carpet, revealing a lady of average height gowned in silver, her thick blond hair looped about her head in heavy braids. She shifted her back, and a double set of round fairy wings unfolded from between her shoulder blades, extending out about six feet. A single round feather, transparent except for its golden tip, fluttered downward to land on the head of a huge white cat that sat at her feet.

The feline looked up at the woman and made a series of short, staccato sounds.

"Oops. I'm so sorry," she said, and the feather burst into dazzling, multicolored particles that promptly vanished. "There." She beamed at Daventry. "Was that an impressive entrance?"

"Rather," he managed to get out.

She stepped forward, the silk of her fashionable

evening dress whispering softly with her movement. "I have come in answer to your wish."

"My—" He stared at her, not quite able to accept what he had just seen.

"Your wish," she repeated. "Do you not remember? You made it a few minutes ago, while looking up at a star. For a wife?" she prompted when he made no answer.

He shook his head.

She sighed. "Oh, dear. Perhaps it was a bit *too* impressive." She took his arm and led him to a sofa, where she pressed him to take a seat. "I didn't mean to startle you. Only I've found people are more willing to believe I'm a fairy godmother if I make it obvious from the beginning."

"A—a fairy godmother," he repeated. He'd had only one glass of wine, hadn't he?

She beamed at him. "That's right. A fairy godmother. And I have come in answer to your wish, to grant you the opportunity to find the perfect wife."

"A fairy godmother." He reached out to touch one of her wings, and another gold-tipped feather drifted toward the floor. He pulled his hand back. "I beg your pardon."

She shrugged her shoulders, the movement dislodging another quill. "It doesn't matter. I have a great many of them." The cat made a noise that sounded like *myap,* and the lady cast it a withering glance. "Very funny," she said.

She turned back to Daventry. "I am Xanthe. You may introduce me to people as Lady Xanthe Simms.

And this," she added, gesturing to her furry companion, "is Titus. He will introduce himself, I make no doubt. Now, you desire a wife, but your estates need constant supervision, making it impossible for you to go to London. Is that right? Well, that makes the solution obvious."

"It does?" The possibility that he suffered from a hallucination occurred to him. It would be the first, though, and this all seemed amazingly real.

"Dear boy, of course I am real." She gave him an indulgent smile. "You will grow accustomed, never fear."

He regarded her in consternation. "You can read my mind?"

"Only when you allow it. Now, I have the most delightful scheme. I feel certain you will approve."

"I will?" He had serious doubts of just about everything at the moment.

A mischievous light danced in her violet eyes. "Indeed you will, dear boy. We shall throw a house party at the Court. Over the Christmas season, I think. Yes, definitely over Christmas. And we shall invite a number of eligible ladies, which will give you the opportunity to make your choice. Will that not be delightful?"

"For whom?" he said before he could stop himself.

"For us all," she pronounced with conviction, and beamed at him once more. "Don't worry. All my godchildren are a trifle confused at first. I can't think why." The laughter sparkled in her eyes.

He straightened. "A house party. I could not possibly hold one here. The state of this place—"

"You may safely leave all that to me. Did you think I would make my decree and then desert you? I shall see to everything. You have only to carry out your part of the bargain we shall make and choose a wife."

"Bargain?" he asked quickly, eyes narrowing.

"It is no great matter. I promise to grant you the opportunity to achieve your heart's desire, and you promise to make the most of that opportunity."

"And if I fail to find a lady to my liking?"

She shook her head, to the imminent peril of her looping braids. "Then you will know you have wasted your opportunity, and must go about meeting a suitable lady in the ordinary manner, by going to London and spending a Season. Would you prefer that?"

"No!" His vehemence surprised him. "No," he repeated more calmly. "I prefer to remain here. And you will arrange this house party, take care of all the details, make all the arrangements, do all the work. Why?"

"Because I love to grant opportunities. Here." She hummed a lilting bar, then held out her cupped hands, revealing a dancing flame between her palms. "Take it, and our covenant is sealed."

He hesitated. "A fairy godmother?"

The cat flicked the tip of its tail.

Xanthe smiled. "A fairy godmother," she agreed. "Come. Are you not willing to try for your heart's desire?"

A sudden longing filled him to believe in this incredible woman. But it seemed impossible his problem could be settled so easily. "I have only to act as host?"

"And I shall be your hostess. We shall entertain our guests, and you will find the lady who will win your heart and bring life and joy back into your home." She extended her hands once more, the flame within them dancing higher as she added softly, "Is that not what you want?"

His military mind rejected the entire situation, but some deeper understanding, some innate recognition that this was indeed truth, filled him with certainty.

Without giving himself time for senseless reflection, he reached out, and the flame leaped from her hands to his. It burned without heat, sending a tingling sensation through his palms and wrists all the way to his elbows, dancing and sparkling with a life of its own. For a moment, it stilled. Then the fire flared, bursting into myriad iridescent lights that vanished before they reached the carpet.

Xanthe's delightful smile flashed. "There, it is settled. Tomorrow I shall ready the house and send out the invitations." She rose. "Shall we go in to dinner now? The others will be waiting for us. And they will not be in the least surprised to see me, for they shall believe I am an old friend of your late stepmamma whom they have been expecting." Her eyes danced with suppressed laughter. "Being a fairy godmother is the most delightful fun."

Two

Miss Desdemona Lynton gazed out the carriage window at the stars, her fertile brain devising schemes of amusement that would undoubtedly dismay her aging, staid father had she ever thought it worth confiding these to him. She glanced at him, but could make out no more than his dim shape, of average height but impressive bulk, where he sat on the rear seat, covered by the fur lap robe to keep off the night chill. She could not discern the details of his impeccable evening dress, nor that of his youngest sister, a spinster of eight-and-twenty, who sat at his side. Dear Aunt Charlotte, so sweet and patient, so eminently capable of dealing with the household of her widowed brother. And so utterly boring.

She turned back to the window, snuggling her feet closer to the brick that had long since lost all vestiges of heat, allowing her mind to wander back over the evening party they had attended at Brompton Towers, seven miles distant. In winter, the country offered limited opportunities for young ladies of quality to indulge in larks. Three highly successful

Seasons and five very flattering proposals of marriage had probably spoiled her for lesser sport.

She sighed and set about the wistful devisement of some project to enliven her days. If only her father would accept the intriguing invitation they had received that morning to join a house party over Christmas at Kellands Court. How she longed to see Lady Xanthe Simms once more.

A slight frown creased her brow, only to fade as the strains of a lilting melody filled her mind. Pity her father had cordially disliked the late earl. She wondered what the son would be like. Nine-and-twenty, and the last eleven years of his life spent with the army at war. A serious gentleman, according to Miss Brompton, who spoke with all the authority of one whose only contact with him had been when her father paid a call of ceremony upon his new neighbor. Aunt Charlotte, she reflected not at all irrelevantly, was eight-and-twenty, and quite serious.

The crunching of gravel as the carriage turned through the massive wrought iron gates and onto the drive of Lynton Park roused her. Lamps glowed along the front of the house, giving the modest Georgian dwelling a welcoming appearance. She yawned, and the pleasant thought of her warm, comfortable bed came to her mind.

Aunt Charlotte stirred, and in the moonlight her gentle smile gleamed. "You've been very quiet, Desdi. Did you not enjoy yourself this evening?"

"It was a trifle flat." Desdi's voice held a note of apology, though she'd spoken with considerable kindness. The party, made up primarily of couples of her father's generation, had been given over to political talk and penny whist, a consummate bore to a lively young lady.

"Splendid evening." Sir Joshua Lynton stifled a yawn, then peered at his front door as the carriage pulled to a halt before it. "Where the devil is Benbridge? He knows I like the door open the moment we pull up." He climbed down without waiting for the footman, who was perched on the box, shivering beside the coachman. Leaving both his sister and daughter to the servant's care, he mounted the steps. "The damned thing is locked!" he exclaimed, and applied the knocker with considerable force.

Desdi, who had followed her aunt from the carriage, raised her eyebrows. "We seem to be in for stormy weather," she murmured.

Aunt Charlotte threw her a worried look. "Oh, I do trust not. So very unwise for him to fly into a pelter. Do you think—"

The flinging wide of the door cut short her question. Benbridge's portly figure stood illuminated in the candlelight that flooded onto the porch. His one hand clutched the jamb, his other he held to his head. Something dark trickled between his fingers. Sir Joshua stared at his butler, speechless.

A soft gasp escaped Aunt Charlotte. Desdi ran lightly up the shallow steps and grabbed the butler's arm. She led him into the broad entry hall, where she shoved him into one of the carved chairs that lined the wall beneath a portrait of one of her grandfather's horses. "What happened?" she demanded.

"Where is everyone?" She dropped to one knee beside the man and examined his head.

Sir Joshua remained in the open doorway, glaring about the room. "I demand to know what the devil has been going on!" he repeated.

"Yes, dear brother, I daresay we shall know soon enough." Aunt Charlotte joined Desdi, then glanced over her shoulder at Sir Joshua. "Will you not try to find Mrs. Benbridge? This is a nasty cut, and he has a swelling on the back of his head as big as a goose egg."

Desdi rose. "I'll go."

"Two men," the butler managed to gasp. "At the kitchen door. Masked. They—they had pistols. They ordered everyone except me into the storeroom and locked them in, then made me come with them to show them where to find the most valuable objects. I tried to take the pistol from one of them, and—" He frowned, his fingers exploring the lump on the back of his skull.

"The other man must have hit you," finished Aunt Charlotte.

"At least he didn't shoot." Desdi hugged herself. "I'd best let the others out, then see what has been stolen. Pappa—" She looked up to find her father standing in the doorway into the dining room, his complexion taking on an alarmingly purplish hue.

"It's an outrage!" he exclaimed. "Damn the local authorities. We need a Runner—and so I'll tell old Coginham."

"He died last summer," Aunt Charlotte reminded him. "Sir William is now magistrate."

Sir Joshua's color darkened even more. "Damned jackanapes. No wonder all's gone to the devil around here. Getting so a man can't even sleep in his bed without fear of being murdered in it." He turned on his heel and strode off, still muttering to himself.

Desdi, pausing only to assure herself Aunt Charlotte could deal with the shaken Benbridge, ran to the kitchen storeroom and released the servants, who had been crowded into the small area. Two of the maids indulged in a fit of the vapors, but Desdi wasted no time on them. After dispatching the housekeeper to the aid of her husband and telling the others not to stand about staring but to make themselves useful, she set forth for a tour of the lower apartments.

She reached the dining room first, for the house had been designed for expedience. She stopped in the doorway, her appalled gaze taking in the tumbled chairs, the sideboards with their doors and drawers cast wide, the linens scattered about the floor. Not so much as a single piece of silver or goldplate glittered in the candlelight that blazed in the room. Yet the thefts mattered little compared to the sense of violation, of intrusion into her safe world.

After a moment, she turned away. A rapid survey of the salons and drawing rooms assured her the housebreakers had made a thorough job of it. They had stripped paintings from the walls, candlesticks from the tables. Only the fine, delicate pieces of china remained; the thieves, it seemed, had no desire to break such things.

She returned to the hall, where dear Aunt Charlotte directed the servants in assisting the injured butler to his quarters. She'd see him well tended, Desdi knew. Already the sounds of straightening emanated from the dining room, indicating her aunt had matters—and the distraught servants—well in hand.

The job had been so thorough, so professional, Desdi doubted the culprits had missed anything. Dreading what she might find—or rather, what she feared she wouldn't find—she mounted the stairs and made her way along the hall to her own chamber. The most valuable pieces of jewelry, of course, remained secure in the locked room at the top of the house. But the ones Desdi treasured the most she had kept in her late mother's trinket case, hidden in a cabinet near her bed.

They'd found it, of course. She hesitated just over the threshold, her gaze on the armoire door someone had forced open, breaking its hinges. Bits of clothing lay scattered on the floor, but the one item she wanted desperately to see was missing.

The rest of the house she had viewed with a sense of shock, as if she, personally, had been touched by those thieving hands, but her undauntable spirit had also accepted what had occurred. This was different. It outraged her that someone could have willfully deprived her of her most loved possession, the marquetry box that had been her mother's. Anger surged within her. She turned on her heel and marched back down the stairs, her mind seething with absurdly impossible plots to discover the identities of the perpetrators and recover her treasure.

She found her father pacing the hall, a glass of brandy in his hand. Aunt Charlotte turned as she reached the landing. "Is it the same upstairs?"

Desdi nodded. "If we set out with lanterns at once, we ought to be able to pick up their trail. The snow is thin, but it has not yet melted."

Her father stopped in his tracks, his heavy brow lowering. "You will do no such thing."

Desdi's hands clenched. "They took Mamma's jewelry box. I *will* have it back."

"Your father is right, my love," Aunt Charlotte said hastily. "We shall have the authorities out as soon as it is light—"

"The tracks will be gone then!" Desdi protested.

"I've sent for Sir William," her father stuck in, his tone testy. "There is nothing more we can do."

Aunt Charlotte replaced a flower that had fallen from its arrangement in a Chinese vase. "It must be the same men who robbed the Towers last week, and old Mr. Ridley's home several days before that."

Sir Joshua gave a short nod. "Which is why we will do nothing without the proper authorities. Desperate men. I won't have you mixing yourself up in it, m'girl. Do you understand me?"

"But—"

"No buts. You will do as you're told, and leave the investigation to those who are trained for such things. Do I make myself clear?"

A shaky breath escaped Desdi. "Perfectly."

He nodded. "You're a good puss. Tell you what. I know it's dull around here for you. Otherwise you wouldn't take such crazy notions into your head. We'll

accept Lady Xanthe's invitation. Head over to Kellands Court tomorrow, as soon as you can get yourself
packed. Have some young people to talk to."

And keep you out of danger. He didn't have to
say the words aloud. Desdi could read them in his
uneasy expression. She started to protest, glanced at
Aunt Charlotte, and hesitated. An earl, after all, was
an earl. A serious-minded earl at that, who just
might take a fancy to a spinster who was well accustomed to managing a household just as a gentleman liked. She cast her gaze downward in a picture
of demure acquiescence. "Very well, Pappa. As you
wish."

Her doting pappa glared at her in suspicion.
"Minx," he muttered and strode from the room.

Desdi peered out the window of the coach as the
vehicle rattled over the pitted drive between a yew
hedge and a row of hawthorn shrubs that had been
allowed to run riot. The rumors of the late earl's
being a cheeseparing old nipfarthing, in the rather
reprehensible words of their kitchen maid, who was
sister to one of the grooms at Kellands, just might
be true. Either that or the estates were grossly encumbered. Rarely had she seen such neglect in a
home whose owner resided there year round.

Her father snorted. "Hasn't had a lick of work
done on it since I laid eyes on it last, nigh on fifteen
years ago. That was when Maria—his second wife—
was still alive."

"The new earl seems to have done something, at

least," Desdi pointed out. "There have been weeds removed. See? You can just make out the holes where they were pulled."

They rounded a bend, and she caught her first glimpse of the rambling Tudor building with its multipaned windows surrounded by ragged ivy that bore silent testimony to the ravages of recently applied clippers. Someone *had* been trying—recently, at least. It was a great pity it hadn't been done earlier.

They pulled up before the door, which opened at once to reveal a liveried footman. The decay of the grounds did not seem to affect the household staff, she noted with approval. She jumped lightly down and looked about, trying to picture Aunt Charlotte as mistress of this establishment. Behind her, her practical relative accepted her brother's aid in descending from the traveling carriage, all the while adjuring him to get in out of the cold, that the wind would do his chest no good. Desdi sighed. Aunt Charlotte showed no proper interest in the house.

She fell into step behind them, following them toward the front door, only to pause at the sight of the ageless lady of medium build, gowned in fashionably flounced bright blue merino, who welcomed Aunt Charlotte with an effusive hug. Delight filled Desdi at seeing Lady Xanthe again, though at the moment she could not quite place their last meeting. But that didn't matter in the least.

Sir Joshua took Xanthe's hand and kissed her cheek, surprising Desdi with the apparent closeness of the friendship. She had never seen her gruff father greet any woman in that manner before. Then Lady Xanthe's laughing violet eyes turned on Desdi, and music seemed to fill her heart.

"Aubrey, dear boy," Xanthe cried. "Come and meet our newest arrivals." She drew Desdi forward.

The earl stepped out of the shadows of the entry hall, and Desdi froze, gazing at him, her heart skipping a beat. That commanding height, the broadness of shoulder and narrowness of hip, those piercing, wide-set hazel eyes and the jutting chin, the crop of closely curling blond hair . . . no flesh-and-blood mortal, this, but her own secret daydream come to life, the ideal image of a gentleman she held close in her heart, the secret reason she had accepted none of the flattering offers she had received.

He took her hand, and his touch warmed her even through the supple kid leather of her glove, proving he was very real. She swallowed, finding her mouth dry. No words came to mind with which to acknowledge Lady Xanthe's introduction. She stared into those wonderful eyes, amber now, flecked with jade.

A spark lit in their depths, as of recognition, a kindred spirit, a carefree, adventure-loving soul.

No, she must have been mistaken, carried away by his startling resemblance to a man who existed only in her dreams. The smile he awarded her held politeness, nothing more. No interest, yet a new tightness settled about his eyes. As of control? she wondered. Had he just made a conscious decision to force back and reject his reaction to her?

That puzzled her. No, more than that. It hurt to be dismissed without his ever allowing himself to explore that spark she had glimpsed. Before she could speak, before she could demand the return of his full attention, he had turned from her, his face closed over as he spoke to Aunt Charlotte, asking about the journey. His smile held no more than formal politeness. It didn't suit him. She longed to see his countenance light with honest amusement.

Lady Xanthe took her arm, and Desdi looked up into the woman's mischievous face. It was ageless, lovely, with a stubborn chin and laughing violet eyes. Desdi smiled back.

"You will want to see your rooms before you meet the others," Xanthe said. "Daventry, will you see to the Marcomes? Thank you, dear boy." She drew Desdi forward, and Aunt Charlotte and Sir Joshua fell in on either side. "I have placed you in the east wing," she told them.

Through an open doorway, Desdi caught a glimpse of a tall young woman in a fashionable green merino traveling gown. She held her head with a regal tilt, enhanced by a neat arrangement of clustered dark curls. The lady turned, granting Desdi a clear view of the classical profile of Lady Eugenia Cumberland. Despite her beauty, she'd never been declared an Incomparable. She held too great a sense of her own consequence to win admiration. But as the years slipped past and no suitable offer had come her way, she had noticeably softened her haughty facade, and Desdi had heard it rumored she would accept a lesser suitor.

There is nothing "lesser" about an earl, Desdi reflected. *This earl, especially.*

They crossed the tiled hall, picking their way through the pile of trunks and portmanteaux that littered the green-and-white marble, and sidestepped the rusting suit of armor that stood guard over the polished oak staircase. Mounting this, they passed an impressive display of tapestries, ancient and tattered from the onslaught of moths. The musty smell of mildew reached her as she brushed past the woven scenes of classical mythology. They could use a good beating.

Oil lamps stood in niches between the hangings, and it dawned on her there was nothing amiss here that a good, thorough cleaning wouldn't set right, and possibly arrangements of flowers or greenery to add a cheering note. It surprised her Lady Xanthe hadn't seen to it.

A girl of about fourteen summers stood in the gallery, watching them with bright, speculative eyes. A wide blue riband tied back her dusky curls at the nape of her neck, and she wore a blue merino dress more suitable to a younger child. Her gaze traveled over Desdi, then settled on Aunt Charlotte with a curiously intent study.

Xanthe introduced Lady Sophronia, then shooed the girl to assist her elder sister with the entertainment of their guests. "So much to do, with everyone arriving," Xanthe exclaimed cheerfully. "Now, Sir Joshua, we have placed you in the Green Room. I believe you will enjoy the view across the pasture."

This did indeed suit Desdi's father, and in minutes they left him to the admiring study of four mares, well along in foal, who grazed on the last remnants of grass.

Xanthe led the way along the corridor, down three steps, around a corner, then stopped before a door leading into a sunny apartment decorated in tones of pink and cream, where Grisham, the abigail shared by Charlotte and Desdi, worried herself over the bestowing of her mistress's dressing case. Desdi followed her hostess to the neighboring room, where ivory and blue dominated the bed and window hangings.

Her luggage had not yet made its way to the apartment, nor would she receive any help until Grisham assured herself of Charlotte's complete comfort. In short, there was nothing for her to do here until the correct valises and trunk arrived. She peered out her window and found she looked down on a formal garden, all very proper and staid, if one overlooked the lack of pruning and weeding. Her gaze traveled beyond to an open parkland, which was much more to her taste. She cast off her bonnet, straightened her hair, and set forth to explore.

Once out her door, she memorized the appearance of the corridor, then headed in the opposite direction from the one in which Lady Xanthe had led them. Her guess proved correct. The first turning brought her within sight of the main staircase. She descended this past the first floor, where the family had their apartments, and down to the great hall.

To her left, she could hear the low babble of voices emerging from behind a closed door, but she had no desire to join them. Instead, she estimated the location of her room, then wandered down a broad hallway. The first door she reached led into a formal drawing room, the next into a dining room with a table capable of seating upward of thirty. Silver gleamed on the mahogany sideboards, but it was the draperied alcove on the far side that caught her attention. She went to it, and was pleased to discover a pair of French windows opening onto a terra cotta tiled terrace bordered by a wrought iron balustrade that overlooked the formal garden.

She slipped out, then wandered along the terrace until she rounded a corner of the house. Here she encountered another set of French doors, and opposite them four shallow steps leading down to the garden path. She descended these.

From somewhere nearby came the tentative, worried meow of a cat in trouble. She stopped, looking about, as the cry rose in volume to a plaintive howl. It came, she determined after the next cry, from a large oak, its branches bare to the winter cold. Halfway along one of its thick limbs, a good ten feet above the ground, a rotund white cat clung as if terrified for its life.

"And what took you up there, sir?" demanded Desdi. "Chasing some poor bird, I suppose."

She strode to the base of the oak and contemplated the feline's plight. He ought to be able to get down with little trouble, but then not all felines possessed the necessary skills. This one might well be as clumsy as her own Hecuba had been, a spoiled lap cat who rarely could be induced to stir outdoors.

The animal eyed her and let loose with a piteous, soulful wail that tugged at her heart. She could hardly leave the poor thing there. Even as she contemplated the situation, the wind picked up and the icy chill of the gathering dusk assailed her. She eyed the sturdy branches once more and came to her decision. Trees had never posed a problem to her in her hoydenish youth. She reached up, found a firm grip, swung herself with gratifying ease into the lower branches, and found a perch on which to sit.

"Here, sir," she called softly to the cat.

It merely dug its claws deeper into the bark and stared at her, its gaze reproachful.

"Are you going to make me come all the way up after you?" she demanded.

Apparently so. The cat made no move to come to her reassuring calls. She balanced herself against the trunk, reached for a higher branch, and worked her way through the limbs until she reached a position where she could almost touch the frightened feline. At least it had stopped its piteous complaints, and now watched her with that look that might either be fascination or complete disapproval. With a cat, one never could be quite certain. She steadied herself, rose so that she mostly stood, and reached out to grasp the cowering bundle of white fur.

The cat, infuriatingly, swarmed farther along the branch, hunkered down, and wrapped its full tail about its feet.

"Beast," Desdi declared. "You did that on purpose."

A crunch on the gravel warned her she was no longer alone. It was followed almost at once by a deep voice.

"And just what do you think you are doing?" Exasperation colored the tone, but it was tinged with amusement.

"Performing a rescue." She could only be glad the man stood behind her and could not see the embarrassed color that flamed in her cheeks. With caution, she eased herself about sufficiently to discover who had caught her in so undignified a position. Through the growing dark, she could make out a tall figure with tightly curling blond hair and a decidedly military stance—her host, the earl himself.

Dismayed, determined to ignore him, she edged forward after the elusive cat. With the next step she missed her footing. For a moment she dangled by one hand, the other grasping frantically for purchase. Then she lost her grip and tumbled from the tree.

Before she could gather herself into a ball to roll, she collided with something far softer than the ground or the tree, yet almost as sturdy. One of the earl's strong arms caught her about the shoulders, the other swept behind her legs, and she found herself pressed tightly against his very broad chest. For a moment she stared at him, stunned, part of her very much enjoying this unexpected turn of events.

He appeared every bit as startled as she, gazing at her with considerable consternation. Something else showed in his eyes, too, something she couldn't quite identify, yet which made her heart beat faster. Yes, she could enjoy this very much indeed.

Abruptly, the gleam vanished from his eyes. "That," he declared with daunting force, "was as foolish and frivolous a piece of behavior as it has ever been my misfortune to witness. It is conduct wholly unbecoming to a young lady."

Desdi, chagrined by his words, opened her mouth to deliver a blistering retort. She stopped, though, as the humorous aspect of the situation came home to her. "It was also," she informed him, mimicking his caustic tone, "quite unnecessary."

She gestured to where the huge white cat descended the tree with a nonchalance that belied its earlier wails. Upon reaching the ground, the immense animal settled on its haunches and proceeded to groom its tousled fur back into place as if that were its only concern in the world.

"You may put me down, as well," Desdi suggested.

Daventry stiffened, as if he had been unaware he still clasped her in his arms. He set her on her feet, gave her a short nod, and strode off the way he must have come, back toward the terrace and that second set of French doors that now stood slightly ajar. Without so much as a backward glance, he disappeared inside. The doors closed behind him with a salutary thud.

A deep sigh escaped Desdi, and she turned to the cat. "I do not believe he is pleased with me."

The feline stopped in its fastidious work on one paw and fixed her with an unblinking, unnerving regard.

"What are you looking at?" she snapped. "I am not pleased with *him,* either." Well, his disapproval of her didn't please her, at least. Yet the memory of his strength and the subtle scents of leather and bay and something more elusive that clung to him continued to tantalize her senses for a very long while.

Three

Daventry stood before the hearth, glaring into the fire he had requested be kindled in the grate. What the devil was that young lady doing here? His fairy godmother could hardly consider *her* a suitable candidate for his wife.

Climbing trees, of all things. That she had been trying to rescue that perverse feline Titus made matters no better. That she had fallen into his arms made them decidedly worse.

He swore softly under his breath and strode across the room, then back again. The memory haunted him of the delightful weight of the girl as he held her, of the scent of violets—and oak—that clung to her, of the startled laughter that lit her large green eyes.

He could not permit himself to be diverted. He needed a capable, practical wife, not some flighty chit forever falling into scrapes. A glance about his disreputable household should prove sufficient reminder. He would waste not so much as a single other thought on Miss Desdemona Lynton. Instead, he would concentrate on the more suitable ladies provided by Xanthe.

He made his way to the Blue Salon, where they were to gather before dinner, and to his surprise found no fire in the grate. In fact, ashes remained from the morning, and no new logs lay beside the hearth. A general feeling of neglect and disarray lay over the whole apartment—and his guests, he realized in consternation, would be coming down in the very near future. He rang the bell and waited in growing impatience until Finley appeared.

As soon as his majordomo entered the apartment, Daventry gestured toward the fireplace. "Why hasn't this been tended?"

Finley's already harassed expression sharpened in repressed irritation. "I shall see to it at once."

"I asked *why* it hadn't been tended already," Daventry pointed out gently. "Are the maids not capable of doing their jobs?"

Finley looked distinctly uncomfortable. "You must not blame Alice, m'lord. Mrs. Whitlaw has had her busy elsewhere."

"Then perhaps I had best speak to Mrs. Whitlaw."

Relief flooded Finley's countenance. "Certainly, my lord. I will ask her to come to you at once."

"She must be busy, indeed, to allow this room, of all places, not to be cleaned." Daventry kept his expression bland. "I believe I shall go to her. Where is she?"

Finley clenched his hands together. "I—I really could not say, my lord."

"I thought not," Daventry muttered. "What's amiss, man?"

Finley cleared his throat. "I believe she was not feeling well."

"I see." Daventry set forth for the housekeeper's room, where he found that lady reclining in a chair, her feet propped on a stool, a novel in her hands, and a cup of tea and plate of biscuits on a table at her side.

She stared at him for a moment, then came slowly to her feet, her cheeks flushed. "My—my lord! You find me taking a much needed rest."

"Indeed," he said and repeated his query concerning the unkempt apartment where his guests would shortly gather.

She gave an artificial laugh. "Lord, I don't know whether I am on my head or my heels, what with all these people in the house. A terrible confusion it is, and the maids that unused to it." She shook her head. "I have to follow every one of them about just to be certain they're doing their jobs. I am quite exhausted with so much extra work."

He arranged his features into a semblance of sympathy. "I hope it isn't proving too much for you?"

She bristled. "No one can keep this great house the way I can, my lord. You are lucky to have me."

"What I would be lucky to have," he pointed out, "would be the salon dusted and made presentable before dinner."

Her mouth thinned, and she sniffed. "I'll not listen to slights. I am a hardworking woman, and if you do not appreciate the job I do, then I shall leave this house. At once," she added, with the smug certainty of one who knew no employer would take her up on such a threat with his establishment filled with guests.

He inclined his head. "As you wish, Mrs. Whitlaw." Only a touch of his anger reached his voice. "I will inform Finley of your decision. You need not delay your departure. I feel certain we will be able to manage until we have found a replacement." He gave her a short nod, turned on his heel, and exited. As he shut the door behind him, he could hear her sputtering—whether in protest or indignation he didn't bother to ascertain.

That left him without a housekeeper. Had he a wife, he could leave the matter of finding a new one in her capable hands. As it was, he had only Xanthe, and he doubted whether she included the hiring of domestic staff as part of her wish granting. He considered begging her to supply a magical servant, but knew that would solve little. He needed a competent—and permanent—woman established in the house, familiar with its routines, before turning it over to a prospective bride.

He returned to the Blue Salon and found Xanthe there before him. All traces of disarray had vanished, as if by magic—which was probably exactly the case. A fire burned cheerfully in the hearth, sending a warming, soothing glow through the room.

At the moment, Xanthe busied herself playing the role of gracious hostess to a tall, thin lady just past the first blush of youth. Fanny Marcome, that was her name. He regarded her critically, noting the stubborn chin and smoothly plaited dark hair. *Neat,* he decided. Probably quite capable of taking on the duties he required of his future wife. His gaze moved on to her father, the retired Colonel Marcome, a stolid gentleman with a permanent scowl. His hatchet-faced wife stood meekly at his side.

The door opened to admit the Eaveslys, a brother and sister a scant year or so younger than himself. Miss Harriet Eavesly, a small, fair creature tending toward a pleasing plumpness, dressed with an elegance more commonly associated with taller, more slender young ladies. She regarded the room with bright, intelligent eyes. When she spoke, her soft words didn't carry to Daventry, but he noted how her brother instantly took her arm and led her toward Xanthe. Managing, it seemed. Another capable young lady.

His duty to his sister completed, George Eavesly headed straight for Daventry and the decanters. The earl handed him a glass, from which the young man took a long, refreshing swallow, followed by another. At last he rocked back on his heels, eyeing the assembling company. "Devilish fine house party, Daventry. It's good to see Lady Xanthe again. Remarkable woman." He cast a sideways glance up at him. "Daresay you don't remember me. At Eaton, though a few years behind you."

Daventry racked his memory and dredged up vague images from the distant past. "Of course," he said.

George Eavesly drained his glass and grinned as

Daventry refilled it. "No need to pretend. Lord, there's no reason you should remember me."

Daventry shook his head. "You played cricket."

George stared at him in open admiration. "Fancy you remembering that."

The door opened again, and Miss Charlotte Lynton entered, followed by Sir Joshua. *Her brother must be nigh on fifteen years older than she,* he reflected, noting her smooth, youthful countenance. She must be about his own age, and Xanthe had said something about her managing her brother's household since the death of his wife eight years before. She'd also had the managing of her niece. Daventry poured himself another glass and studied her more closely. She certainly had the sort of experience he sought in a wife. Her gentle countenance showed no sign of weakness, and her remarkably fine eyes lent her a loveliness that would last her entire life.

Then the door burst wide, and in swept Miss Desdemona Lynton in a cloud of peach muslin that set off her dusky ringlets. Laughter seemed to fill the room, swirling in with her, emanating from her. She went at once to George Eavesly, greeting him like an old friend.

It took several minutes before Daventry realized she had not come in alone. Lady Eugenia Cumberland, a straight-backed young lady in a beruffled gown of pink lutestring, now stood at Xanthe's side. At her elbow hovered her father, the earl of Lowestoft, a frail Tulip in a pale green coat nipped in at the waist, with numerous fobs crossing his brocade waistcoat and an emerald gleaming in the elaborate folds of his lace-edged neckcloth.

After distributing more glasses of wine, Daventry strolled among his guests, exchanging greetings. *An oddly assorted lot,* he reflected, though all seemed quite pleasant. Their only common ground seemed to be the possession of an eligible female in their immediate family. He paused as he reached Colonel Marcome, his gaze straying to Miss Charlotte Lynton, who had stood in serious conversation with the older man. The colonel looked up, gave Daventry a short nod, and excused himself.

Miss Lynton watched him wander off with a smile, then turned to regard Daventry with a considering expression in her eyes. "Mr. Doncaster speaks highly of you," she said in a low and well-modulated voice.

He inclined his head. "I am flattered. Are you well acquainted with our rector, then?"

"He serves a parish of more than twenty square miles, poor man. It includes Lynton Park. I was so very glad for him when Mr. Beardsley came to be his curate last summer."

"Then perhaps you will be pleased to know both will be joining us for dinner tonight."

Her smile warmed. "Indeed, I shall be delighted to see them."

He regarded his companion with a measure of approval. She spoke like a sensible woman, showing a concern for matters beyond her own household, a kindness toward other people. A countess needed such qualities to endear her to those bound to her husband's estates. She might do very well as his wife. Her only drawback, in fact, was her close relationship to Miss Desdemona Lynton.

He frowned as the girl once more thrust herself into his mind. He'd been avoiding her, carefully not looking to where she stood among her fellow guests, trying not to listen to the lilting sound of her frequent laughter. It was only natural, he assured himself, that after so many years of warfaring he should find himself attracted to so much light and life. A fleeting attraction, nothing more. It was not to be considered in the serious business of selecting a suitable wife.

Finley entered, at his most formal, and in imposing accents announced the arrival of the Reverend Mr. Doncaster and the Reverend Mr. Beardsley. Daventry stepped forward to greet the elderly rector, whom he had known since childhood, then turned to the curate, who hovered solicitously at his superior's elbow. He made the necessary introductions to those few guests who did not already know them. Within moments of these newest arrivals receiving their glasses of Madeira, Finley returned to announce that the meal was served.

This was the first dinner party over which he had presided, and Daventry found it both amusing and alarming. He looked down the length of the table to where Xanthe fulfilled the role of his hostess, seated between Colonel Marcome and Lord Lowestoft. Frederick, too, performed his part as assistant host to perfection, keeping both Miss Charlotte Lynton and Lady Lowestoft well entertained.

Daventry glanced at Mrs. Marcome, who sat on his right, but she remained in conversation with young George Eavesly. Lady Eugenia, on Daventry's left, currently spoke to Sir Joshua. That gave him a respite, for which he found himself heartily grateful. So far, Mrs. Marcome had missed no opportunity to point out her daughter's many excellent qualities, which only served to make the poor girl sound a dead bore. Nor had he found conversation with Lady Eugenia any less daunting, for she seemed to enjoy making blunt comments, not always complimentary, about her fellow guests.

He allowed his gaze to drift to Miss Fanny Marcome, who listened with proper attentiveness to some comment made by Lord Lowestoft. Perhaps her matchmaking mamma didn't exaggerate that much. She seemed an admirable young woman, whose only apparent flaw lay in the fact she had remained a daughter of her household for too long, without the opportunity to take over the duties and responsibilities of being its mistress. He considered the possibility that she might be a touch vapid, then decided to postpone judgment. He would have to converse with her again, for her lack of animation might simply spring from nerves or shyness rather than any lack of intelligence or humor.

His gaze roved around the table, only to pause as he reached Miss Desdemona Lynton. Now, there was a rare handful. How could so tiny a person contain so much life and spirit? She had weighed so little, yet proved such a delectable armful—

No, that line of thought took him to places it

would not be advisable for him to go. He forced
his gaze to travel on to her aunt, Miss Charlotte
Lynton. One could not help but notice the elegant
carriage of that fine head on its slender neck, or
the graceful manner in which she drew one conversation to a close and turned to the gentleman on her
other side. The role of hostess would come naturally
to her, as did that air of sober propriety. Possibly
she had cultivated it as a defense in bringing up that
hoydenish niece of hers.

Here his glance strayed to Desdemona Lynton
again and found her engulfed in a mirth she tried
unsuccessfully to hide. As both George Eavesly and
Bertie Cumberland, Lady Eugenia's brother, also
struggled to maintain their countenances, they appeared to be sharing a joke. Daventry wished someone would repeat it so he could hear. The meal had
grown somewhat tedious.

It drew to a close at last, and the ladies followed
Xanthe from the dining room. She would take them
to the formal drawing room, Daventry suddenly realized with a sinking heart. A harp occupied that
room, as did a pianoforte. That undoubtedly meant
he would shortly have each young lady's particular
talent flaunted before him. He forced back an involuntary shudder. He enjoyed music, always had—but
not the sort most likely to be found at house parties.

And his half sisters would be there. Sophie had
been thrilled at being allowed to be present. Bella,
though, had been too busy sulking at having been
excluded from the dinner party. When he'd told her
she would be joining them soon enough, she had

merely sniffed and taken herself off in a flounce of skirts.

He allowed the gentlemen to linger over their port, but not too long. As much as the craven impulse might appeal to him, he could not neglect the ladies on this first night. When the decanter had passed one more time, he suggested they join them, and Daventry and the other gentlemen—with Mr. Eavesly taking one last massive swallow that left him choking—trooped through to the adjoining apartment.

As they entered, Xanthe looked up from the pianoforte, where the dusky-haired Lady Eugenia Cumberland took her seat before the keyboard. The fairy's wicked smile flashed, and she strolled over to lay her hand on Daventry's arm. "There is no need to scowl so, dear Aubrey." Her laugh sounded softly in his ear.

"Do I? I beg your pardon. I fear my years with the army have not prepared me for this current engagement."

Those mischievous violet eyes sparkled. She hummed a lively bar or two, and suddenly Lady Eugenia wore the uniform of a French dragoon. The other guests displayed similar changes in costume, members of Belgian, Austrian, Russian, and even British units. The fire no longer burned in the hearth, but in a circle of stones. Against the far wall stood a picket line with four horses tied to it.

The earl stiffened, disoriented, then drew in a shaky breath. "Very realistic," he murmured. "Are they as they appear? As my enemies or allies?"

She laughed. "No, my dear Aubrey. I only sought to provide a variety." Her gleaming eyes narrowed. "You would see them all in French uniforms, though, would you not?"

He shook his head. "I recognize my need to marry."

"Need," she repeated. "And what of your desire?"

"I *desire*," he emphasized the word slightly, "to see my household in order and my sisters suitably chaperoned."

"And you envision only duty, with no chance for pleasure?" Her gaze held amused sympathy. "Then it will be a battle, indeed."

The uniforms—and livestock—vanished, leaving the guests as they had appeared before. He watched her move away to speak to Lady Lowestoft, but before he could dwell on her words, a high-pitched giggle informed him that the schoolroom party had joined them, and Bella and Sophie had found a kindred spirit in the lively Miss Desdemona Lynton. They sat at a table in the farthest corner, with Miss Lynton and Frederick spreading out the jackstraws for what might well prove a diverting game, judging from Miss Lynton's attempts to arrange the sticks in impossible stacks. Behind him, he could hear the polished performance of Lady Eugenia, but his attention remained on the younger members of the party.

Sophie shrieked with delight, then cast an alarmed look toward him. His brow lowered. The girls showed signs of standing in some awe of him, and he could not understand why. Their notes and letters over the long years of his absence had shown his efforts to remain in contact with them had been worthwhile. They had greeted him warmly enough on his return. It must be that they had not been accustomed to being brought to book for their indiscretions, or having anyone insist upon some measure of propriety. Miss Lynton could use a little discipline herself. She seemed to be encouraging the very sort of behavior he tried to discourage in his sisters.

Applause started, and he became aware that the music had come to an end. He joined politely, but before he could seek a chair, Mrs. Marcome grasped his arm and desired him to turn the pages for her dearest Fanny. He considered declining on the grounds that his duties as host could not be neglected, but the whole purpose of this party was for him to become better acquainted with the ladies selected by Xanthe. Nobly, he took his position.

Miss Marcome played the opening chords, then looked speakingly up into his face. "This is very kind of you," she said, her voice soft and lilting. "I fear I am sadly out of practice."

Her performance, he noted, was flawless, but as sedate and proper as her manners. She would probably make an excellent countess. He murmured a compliment and returned her to her beaming mamma, but before another young lady could be put on display, Xanthe suggested they turn their attention to cards.

Most of the guests, he had already discovered with relief, seemed to be well acquainted. This left him with little to do but assure himself that all found suitable partners. He brightened even further when he realized he would not be needed at the whist table, which held the elderly Reverend Mr. Doncaster and Sir Joshua Lynton, along with Colonel Marcome and Lord Lowestoft.

Xanthe busily organized the matrons of the party into a game of silver loo. Frederick and the curate Mr. Beardsley sat with the schoolroom party, along with Miss Charlotte Lynton and her niece Desdemona. Young Mr. Bertie Cumberland induced Harriet Eavesly into playing at piquet with him. George Eavesly had already drawn Lady Eugenia to one of the smaller tables, which left Daventry with nothing to do but request Miss Fanny Marcome to indulge him in a hand.

He found her to be an uninspiring partner, playing predictably to his leads and showing no flashes of inspiration. He was relieved when she excused herself at the end of their game and joined George Eavesly. This left Daventry with Lady Eugenia, who showed a tendency to deliver measured opinions on such subjects as the weather and the upcoming Season, making him long for silence.

As the hour grew late, he excused himself from Miss Harriet Eavesly, his current partner, and tended to the unpleasant duty of sending his sisters to bed. They went, but with many a backward glance and sighs intended to convey their sense of ill usage.

He felt a trifle ill used himself. Despite the innumerable hands he had played, he had enjoyed very few. The arrival of the tea tray would provide a welcome diversion, for that would allow him to bring to an end this tiresome evening.

He glanced over to where Frederick now played with Miss Charlotte Lynton. They seemed deep in some fascinating discussion, for neither paid any heed to the cards they held. That surprised him. Since the loss of his arm, Frederick had retired into himself, losing his confidence, becoming tongue-tied in the presence of personable females. At the moment, he spoke with considerable animation.

Miss Desdemona rose from her hand with the curate and looked around. Her gaze came to rest on him, and she eyed him speculatively as she strolled over to join him. "Your cousin says you have uncanny luck at piquet."

He inclined his head. "And do you?" He kept his tone polite, with just a hint of discouragement. He found it difficult to know how to hold a lively young lady at a distance, since he had spent his entire adulthood in the company of far from genteel men.

She seemed oblivious to his attempt. She merely awarded him an impish grin as she led the way to a table. "I believe in making my own luck."

In spite of himself, his lips twitched. "My dear Miss Lynton, I should warn you that remark could be taken in more than one way." He seated himself and picked up the reduced deck.

Her eyes danced, belying her look of shocked affront. "I do not fuzz the cards," she informed him in haughty tones as she settled across from him.

"Not for lack of ability, I'll wager," came his prompt response.

"No," she admitted cheerfully. "But it is so much more entertaining to see which of my opponents will try that trick."

His hands, which had been shuffling the pasteboards, paused in their rapid movements. "Has that been tried this night?"

"Only once, and not very expertly." She waved that aside. "I've found people's various approaches to the game to be far more interesting."

"Have you, indeed?" His gaze rested on her as he dealt. "And what has struck you in particular?"

"The rector plays in a style as meandering as his sermons," came her prompt response.

"And Mr. Beardsley?"

She shook her head. "I have yet to have the privilege of hearing him preach, but it should be an enjoyable experience."

"Clever?" Daventry's eyebrows rose.

"Possibly a match for you," she added as he took the final trick of their game, rousting her soundly.

"And my cousin?" he pursued as he began to shuffle once more.

"Ah. Captain Grayson is a gentleman. He assured I should win, but quite discreetly—which is something I would be bound you would never do," she added, eyeing her new cards with disfavor.

He hesitated over his discard, his gaze resting on her. "Would you rather be allowed to win?"

She wrinkled her nose. "Never," she declared, then demanded three cards to replace those she rejected.

It occurred to him to ask what she learned about

him from his manner of play, but he thought better of it. Her opinion might prove too disconcerting.

The tea tray arrived at last, and Xanthe took her place behind it. For some time, he was occupied with helping pass out cups and with supplying his male guests with more potent refreshment. At last he took a seat by the young curate and inquired how long he'd been in the neighborhood.

Mr. Beardsley set down his cup. "Almost five months now. Long enough to appreciate your arrival at Kellands Court. Your estate manager has been telling us of the improvements that have already been set under way."

"There should be enough to keep us busy for some time to come," Daventry said, dryly.

Sir Joshua caught his eye, and when Daventry joined him, he demanded, in his bluff way, "Was my girl playing off her tricks on you at piquet? Should never have taught her, I suppose, but she's a quick learner with a lively mind."

"She behaved with perfect propriety," Daventry assured him, then caught the look of relief in her doting pappa's eye. Just what had he expected the young lady to be about? He stepped back. "I hope you and your sister will enjoy the party."

"Oh, as to that, Charlotte has quiet tastes. Just give her something to occupy her, and she'll be happy. Splendid organizer. Don't know what I would have done without her since my wife died. Sacrificed her life for me, which is damned unfair." He shook his head. "Nothing would make me happier than to see her suitably established in a household of her own."

No subtlety there, Daventry noted with amusement. Yet he liked the man's open manner. What he didn't like was this feeling of being hunted.

His gaze traveled to where Miss Charlotte Lynton sat beside Xanthe, and he blinked. The Aubusson carpet had vanished from the floor, and in its place grew a thick lawn of velvety grass. Daffodils and hollyhocks bobbed gently in a nonexistent breeze, and a blanket of sweet william and bluebells spread across the sofa and chairs. A robin landed on his shoulder, then took off to join a dozen others in an aerial ballet above the guests' heads. Xanthe, it seemed, grew bored.

He started to take a sip from his cup, and found himself staring at a tiny golden fish with long sweeping fins. He set it down abruptly. The damned thing wasn't real, of course. None of it was. Yet he found it disconcerting, lacking in any logical order.

The rector and his curate took their leave after drinking a single cup, and several of the ladies expressed their desire to retire. Bertie Cumberland suggested a game of billiards, and the gentlemen departed for the large room devoted to those tables. Daventry started to follow, but stopped as Xanthe reappeared after escorting Lady Lowestoft to her chamber.

"You did not like my little display," she accused.

"I find it unsettling," he admitted. "You are quite certain no one else can see your—your efforts?"

"No one at all. Unless you'd like them to?" she suggested brightly.

"No!"

She shook her head. "I imagine your sisters would be amused."

"My sisters are amused by almost everything."

"Almost," Xanthe agreed.

He looked at her sharply. "What is that supposed to mean?"

But he knew. He didn't need the steady gaze of her violet eyes to remind him he was failing as a brother, even as he tried so very hard to succeed. He turned away and followed his male guests to the sanctuary of the billiards room.

Titus nestled in the center of Xanthe's bed, his feet tucked neatly under his bulk, his tail curled about them, watching the fairy. She hovered in a sitting position before her dressing table while her thick fair hair plaited itself into a long braid down her back. A violet bow appeared at its end, fastening it.

She studied her reflection a moment; then a lace night cap appeared on her head. She nodded in satisfaction and turned to her companion. "You don't have to look quite so disapproving."

Titus blinked sleepy eyes.

"Of course he's having trouble adjusting. He's a man, isn't he? And a military one, at that. He's far too accustomed to settling matters with a curt order."

Titus opened his mouth, and a series of staccato sounds emerged.

"To you?" Xanthe's eyes brimmed with merriment. "I would have liked to see that. And what did he do when you ignored him?"

One white ear flicked, and Xanthe laughed. "Poor Aubrey. I doubt he ever had a cat to deal with in the army, nor little sisters."

Titus cocked his head, and the softest of sounds escaped him.

"His life has been too serious. He has forgotten how to have fun. Even his cousin Frederick has remarked upon it. And you would think that if either man had reason for somberness, it would be Frederick."

Titus directed a pointed stare at her.

Xanthe frowned. "Perhaps you are right. He abandoned his war when he lost his arm. Aubrey still fights his, for he knows no other way to live."

She floated toward the window, and the curtains swept back at her approach. Outside, myriad stars, brilliant and cold, gleamed in the midnight blackness of the sky. Under her thoughtful gaze, and encouraged by her soft humming, they left their natural positions, forming themselves into images of two gladiators, each armed with a giant sword. One struck, the other raised his mighty weapon to parry it, and thunder rumbled across the sky as the blades clashed. The impact shattered them, and the stars that had formed them flew apart. The warriors, too, collapsed as each shining point returned to its proper position. For a long moment, Xanthe remained where she hovered, gazing into the sky that showed no more traces of her handiwork. With a deep sigh, she turned back into the room.

Titus watched her with that skeptical, patient look he so often wore on their jobs.

Her lips twitched. "If it is warfare with which he is comfortable, then perhaps we can ease him into a more normal life with a little war game." Her eyes sparkled. "Come, Titus. We have a great deal of work ahead of us."

Four

Desdi, wrapped in her pelisse, a soft wool scarf draped about her neck, stood at the paddock fence, watching the four mares heavy in foal as they trotted toward their pasture. Three grooms, who had just released the mares from the warm stalls, turned back to their work. The sun had risen above the trees, and the mares stretched out their gleaming necks. Muscles rippled along their sleek flanks, as if their very hairs welcomed the warming rays.

Desdi leaned her head back, breathing in the fresh, crisp air, then turned away, restless. Most of the other ladies of the party sat indoors, embroidering or practicing their music. The gentlemen had embarked upon a ride about the estate.

She would have enjoyed that, but it would have been presumptuous of her to join them, as Daventry had somewhat pointedly excluded the ladies from his invitation. Bertie Cumberland had declined, but she had no taste for his vapid company. On the whole, she wished her pappa hadn't dragged her here. She'd be having much more fun investigating the thefts that had taken place. If it weren't just like her father to rush her away from where anything interesting occurred.

A deep sigh escaped her. She felt certain Lady Arabella, and most particularly Lady Sophronia, could direct her toward some lark or expedition, but the two girls had been consigned to the strict care of a newly acquired governess, who had them hard at work upon their lessons. Life, she decided, could be terribly unfair.

Aimlessly, she set forth on a long, rambling walk, past the outbuildings of the home farm, until she came upon a path bordered with low shrubs, leafless now in the winter cold, but obviously marking a much used walkway—at least much used at one point in time. It didn't seem to have been trod of late. The dried remnants of summer and autumn weeds made traversing the trail more of a challenge, but a mood to explore gripped her, so she lifted the hems of her skirt and pelisse and set forth. Very soon she was glad of the leather gloves she wore, for she was forced to drag back handfuls of the dried stalks to allow herself to pass.

She had gone perhaps three quarters of a mile when the noise of water running over rocks reached her, and she rounded the massive trunk of a gnarled oak to see a narrow stream. Miniature mounds of snow lingered where the sun had not yet penetrated through the tangled branches and undergrowth. An ancient wooden footbridge, still sturdy, assured a safe passage. Desdi crossed it, pleased to find it stable, and continued along the trail.

The village must be in this direction, she realized,

and wondered whose land she crossed. She had no idea of the size of Kellands, or its exact location with respect to the neighboring properties. Then she emerged from a thicket to find herself facing a high shrubbery wall. A low gate led into a courtyard that stood before a stone stable. Beyond it soared the steeple of the church.

She had found the rectory. Pleased, she followed a path that led along the hedge toward what was most likely the front entry to the brick house, but the country voices of several men, probably villagers, reached her. The rector's slow, rambling tones answered them. Then Mr. Beardsley's tenor joined in, his voice reassuring, only to be answered by a rumbling protest from the villagers. *Not a good time to drop in for a visit,* Desdi decided, and turned to make her way back to the Court.

The gentlemen's horses filled the stable, she noted when she at last reached there herself. She must have been exploring for some time. She suspected she looked it, too. Mud splattered the hem of her skirt, despite her attempts to hold it out of harm's way. More soiled her half boots, and her face probably was none too clean, either. She headed for a side door, the one she had used the previous evening when that dratted cat had lured her into attempting a rescue.

She didn't see the cat this time. Instead, Aunt Charlotte emerged from the house, followed closely by Daventry. As the two reached the terrace, Daventry offered Charlotte his arm and escorted her toward the shrubbery.

Desdi hung back beside the hawthorn hedge that gave her shelter. The earl seemed quite attentive. And Aunt Charlotte? She studied her relative's retreating figure. *Shy,* she decided. But the jaunty set to her shoulders implied she was also highly flattered.

An odd sensation seeped through Desdi, of depression, of irritation, of—of jealousy? That was absurd. It could be nothing more than disappointment. Something about the earl, something he kept well buried, had appealed to her. If he preferred to keep it that way, then she shared nothing with him. She had no excuse to do anything other than rejoice that her beloved aunt appeared to be making such a distinguished conquest. Repeating that several times only served to depress her more, and she made her way to her room with very little enthusiasm for tidying her appearance.

Her spirits remained low throughout the afternoon, a situation so unusual as to cause her father to ask uneasily if she were sickening for something. She denied this indignantly, then set about proving it by entering into every conversation with an enthusiasm she found exhausting. It was with relief that she greeted the ladies' withdrawal from the dining room after dinner, and she wondered how soon she could slip away to her chamber.

As soon as she entered the adjoining drawing room, though, Sophie pounced upon her. "You have been this age!" the girl cried, leading her toward the far end of the apartment, where Bella sat before a table, papers spread out about her. "We are trying to devise word games for the rest of the party. Do say you will help."

She did, and was seconded in this effort a short time later by George Eavesly when the gentlemen rejoined the ladies. Daventry, she noted with a sigh, paid them no heed. His duties as host kept him busy, of course, moving from one group of people to another, arranging cards for those who wished to play, speaking to everyone—everyone, that was, except her. For her, he spared no more than a glance. He probably thought of her as a member of the schoolroom party. She hunched a shoulder and concentrated on devising a truly fiendish cipher that would take her victims considerable thought to solve.

Still, her gaze returned to the earl, marking well the words he exchanged with each of the unmarried ladies in the party. She observed Lady Eugenia's simper, Fanny Marcome's blushing stammer, Harriet Eavesly's considered discourse, and Aunt Charlotte's charming laugh. It was no wonder the earl lingered at her aunt's side.

Desdi cast a surreptitious glance across the room to see her father watching his sister and her companion with a satisfied smile. Her dear, doting pappa, whose concern it had always been to find *her* a worthy match. The only reason for him to be so pleased with this situation would be that he must realize Daventry would not have the slightest interest in Desdi.

She returned her gaze to where the earl still stood beside Aunt Charlotte. His interest had to be more than a host's politeness to a guest. In truth, if staid

Aunt Charlotte was the sort of female to whom he was attracted, then he would never look at Desdi. But he'd already made his disinterest in her abundantly plain when she'd fallen out of that silly tree.

She was roused from her depression to find Captain Frederick Grayson had joined their table. The girls greeted him with obvious delight, Sophie with a demand for his opinion on the cipher she struggled to concoct. He settled himself at the girl's side and turned his full attention to the problem.

She liked the captain, Desdi decided. He did not seem to permit the loss of his arm to impair his good humor. He was a year or two older than his cousin, yet he didn't appear as weighed down by as many cares, and the girls obviously adored him. That spoke volumes for his kindly nature.

He smiled abruptly and displayed a simple change to Sophie. "Perfect!" the girl cried, and gave him an enthusiastic hug, far more at ease with her cousin than with her half brother. "You are the best of dear cousins, Frederick."

Bella looked up. "Let me see, Frederick." She took the paper from him, scanned it, and laughed. "How clever you are!"

Captain Grayson ruffled her hair, then turned to look at the assembled guests. A solemn expression crept over his normally amused countenance, rousing Desdi's curiosity. She followed the direction of his gaze and realized he watched Aunt Charlotte, who sat beside Lady Lowestoft, conversing while they both embroidered. Good heavens, her maiden aunt had made a conquest of Captain Grayson, as well.

* * *

Daventry stood before his front door, watching the last of the carriages carry his guests off on a pleasure jaunt into Lincolnshire. They should be gone most of the day, which meant he could turn his attention to the tenanted farms. Mr. Charburton, his agent, had been waiting this half hour past in the estate office, and it was with a feeling of elation that Daventry turned to join him.

He'd had no idea how time consuming would be the demands of a house party. But in one respect, Xanthe had been right in proposing it. He was here where he was needed, instead of being dragged away to distant London, and he'd met several eligible females, any of whom would do an admirable job as his countess.

As he made his way down the hall, he reflected on the several excellent qualities possessed by each of the ladies Xanthe had selected for his inspection. Yet marriage was something he had no desire to leap into without due reflection, in spite of the fact that speed was indeed necessary.

Bella was right—she should have been brought out during the Little Season. And the house—well, Xanthe had made improvements, but it needed more, much more. This wasn't his fairy godmother's home, and she couldn't make the sort of impact on it that it needed, that a real mistress would.

Any of the ladies could fill the role.

Well, any except that flighty little Desdemona Lynton. Sudden amusement rippled through him at the memory of the girl hanging from a limb in the old oak, then losing her grip and falling . . . right into his arms.

Disturbing sensations rippled through him, as powerful as when he'd first clasped her close. She'd been a delight to hold, he couldn't deny that, a delight that would not bear repeating. He could think of no one less suitable for the position of his wife, which made the desires that flared through him equally unsuitable.

The devil with this business of finding a wife. It took his attention too much away from the neglected estate.

As he neared the office, he heard rapid footsteps hurrying in his wake. He turned to see Finley in pursuit of him and waited, his heart sinking at what would undoubtedly prove to be another interruption.

His majordomo caught up, then stood for a moment catching his breath. "Three—three applicants for the position of housekeeper have just arrived, my lord," the elderly man managed at last.

"The devil," Daventry muttered. He knew nothing about domestic matters. If he had a wife, of course—but he'd been over all that with himself. He did *not* have a wife, and that fact did nothing to qualify him to select a female to oversee the smooth running of his establishment. He fixed Finley with a considering eye. "I can think of no one more aware of the problems and needs of the Court. Why do you not perform the interviews and make the decision?"

The man's face blanched. "I—I will endeavor to

give satisfaction, of course, if you truly wish me to try, but—"

"I do. Good man." Daventry clapped him on the shoulder. "You will do a better job than I would," he added with a burst of candor, and escaped to join his estate agent.

He had been working with Mr. Charburton for no more than half an hour when Finley returned to announce the arrival of the Reverends Mr. Doncaster and Mr. Beardsley. Daventry muttered an oath under his breath and made his way to the Blue Salon, where the rector and curate awaited him. At this rate, he reflected with growing irritation, he would never accomplish anything.

Mr. Doncaster struggled to his feet as the earl entered, and came forward with shaky steps to take Daventry's hand. Mr. Beardsley sprang to his superior's side at once, his hand hovering near the elderly man's elbow in a solicitous manner. "So good of you to see us," declared the rector.

Daventry managed a polite smile. "No distressing news, I trust? No more houses robbed?"

"Houses? Robbed?" murmured Mr. Doncaster.

"No," Mr. Beardsley assured him. "For which we are extremely grateful."

The rector, seizing on a concept he understood, nodded. "It is always good to be grateful." Then his brow clouded. "Grateful, but concerned, as well. So many matters that require our attention in the parish. Such a relief for us to know you are now in charge at the Court."

Daventry, with a strong suspicion of what was to

come, ushered them back to their seats. Finley entered carrying a tray on which rested a decanter and three glasses. Robert, the senior footman, followed him, bearing plates of biscuits and sliced nut cakes.

"Such a pleasure to have a man who understands the needs of his fellow creatures," went on Mr. Doncaster, "and is so disposed to look with compassion upon them. Oh, dear me, yes. Most kindly, I feel certain. Not to say anything against your late father, rest his soul. Most unchristian that would be. Most distressing. But so many needs, so many years of neglect, what with the door sticking and the roof leaking and the windowpanes rattling every time there's the least breeze. And it's been such a windy season, has it not? And the rain quite pouring into the church, and the parishioners forced to sit between the buckets and to watch their heads. Not that so many of them are coming as I could wish. And I preached such a very good sermon, did I not, my dear Mr. Beardsley? Quite one of my favorites, all about love and generosity, and that bit from the Book of Matthew I like so much. You remember the bit, don't you? Something about—" He broke off, his gray brow furrowing as he gazed vaguely into space.

Daventry looked to Mr. Beardsley. "The church needs a new roof?"

Mr. Beardsley's engaging smile flashed. "The parishioners have stopped coming, I fear, because they are drenched in their pews in this inclement weather we have had."

Daventry nodded, but absently. He thought he'd

given money for the roof to be repaired shortly after his return home. He'd have to check with his agent, but he was almost positive. And if Mr. Doncaster hadn't used the funds for the roof, what had he done with them? Yet the need was obviously great, which left him to devise a different method of dealing with it. After a moment, he said, "I'll try to have some workmen out there before evening."

"You need not inconvenience yourself," Mr. Beardsley said quickly. "There are several men from the village who would be glad of the work. It will be no trouble for me to engage their services."

Daventry nodded. "You may tell them to submit their fees to my agent, and we will take care of them."

"You are too kind," Mr. Beardsley assured him, but a tightness lingered about his mouth.

Did he prefer the church to be seen paying for church matters? Daventry had no desire to appear the great lord of the neighborhood, yet he could think of no way to discreetly disburse the funds into Mr. Beardsley's keeping without hurting the good rector's feelings. He turned to Mr. Doncaster. "If your workmen know their job, your roof will be fixed before next Sunday."

The rector blinked. "What? Fixed? What will be fixed?"

Mr. Beardsley stood, assisting Mr. Doncaster to his feet as well. "I'll tell you all about it on the way home," the curate said, and took his leave of Daventry.

With a sigh of relief, the earl returned to the estate office, where the daunting list of necessary repairs awaited him. It seemed he would have the opportunity to disburse more of the funds his late father had merely hoarded. Much to his agent's pleasure, he gave orders to begin work on the worst of the tenanted farm houses.

Still, he felt separated from the work, as if he were merely a member of the War Department who remained distant, running the battles from an office a thousand miles away. He preferred the role of a serving line officer. He wanted to be in the thick of the activity.

All too soon he heard the carriages pull up, and once more he was forced to set aside the labors of the estate and tend to the entertainment of his guests. Yet still he lingered until Xanthe came in search of him, drawing him away with her. He managed an almost convincing smile. "I hope everyone enjoyed themselves?"

"I fear several of the young ladies were disappointed you did not make up one of the party, in spite of dear Frederick's efforts to keep them amused." She threw him a mischievous smile. "I see Finley is interviewing a rather large, capable-looking woman. Do you believe she will answer?" She moved ahead. Butterflies fluttered about her, then turned into sparkles that drifted to the carpeted floor and vanished with tiny flashes.

She seemed so unconcerned. If he could call on magic to entertain others or take care of tiresome jobs or turn his home into a smooth running and comfortable haven—the possibilities tantalized him.

But he would lose Xanthe's assistance all too soon, so he had best take all necessary steps to maintain order without magical intervention.

Before he mounted the stairs to dress for dinner that night, he had the satisfaction of feeling he progressed in the right direction. Mrs. Seymour, the candidate approved by Finley, had presented herself to him, assured him she could take up her residence by that evening and her duties by the following morning, and excused herself to set all in train.

He wondered briefly about checking references, but surely the agency had taken care of that detail before ever sending her out to be interviewed. Perhaps the house would run more smoothly now and he could turn his attention to the business of selecting a bride.

As he entered his chamber to find his batman waiting impatiently for his arrival, he couldn't help but wonder what scheme Xanthe would have devised to occupy their guests this night.

He found out all too soon. As the gentlemen joined the ladies in the Ivory Drawing Room after dinner, he knew at once something was afoot. He eyed the eager faces of Miss Eavesly and Miss Marcome, and the delighted ones of his two sisters, and turned at once on Xanthe. "What are you about?" he demanded.

"The most delightful scheme," cried Lady Lowestoft.

Daventry knew a serious foreboding.

"Christmas Eve is almost upon us," Xanthe explained, her expression almost prim. "We have decided to provide our own entertainment."

"We shall perform skits for each other's enjoyment," cried Fanny Marcome with a giggle.

"And we shall devise suitable costumes," added Harriet Eavesly.

"A rare treat, indeed," Daventry agreed, struggling not to reveal his dismay.

Xanthe watched him with that mischievous glint in her violet eyes, then held up a curious shallow basin of chased silver with a mirrored interior. "The ladies shall draw the names of the gentlemen who shall be their partners."

"And what skits are we to perform?" Daventry inquired. This, he presumed, would solve his dilemma of choosing a wife. If he knew anything of Xanthe, she would pair him with the lady of her choice to give him a chance to come to know her. All in all, an excellent scheme, he supposed, except he had never been comfortable performing in front of others.

"What a lark!" cried Bertie Cumberland. "I've always fancied myself an actor!"

"The next Keane, in fact," stuck in George Eavesly.

"Keane?" exclaimed Lady Eugenia with true sisterly feeling. "Bertie cannot even be convincing at charades!"

Amid the exclamations and laughter of the guests, Xanthe walked to Lady Eugenia and offered her the bowl. A lilting melody filled Daventry's mind. Humming? Yes, Xanthe hummed. His suspicions solidified.

Lady Eugenia reached in, then hesitated a moment before withdrawing a folded slip of paper. She opened it, and her face took on a frozen expression. The next moment, she smiled brightly. "It seems we are to be partners, Sir Joshua."

An expression of alarm flitted across Sir Joshua's face before he could arrange his features into a smile. "A delight, my dear. An absolute delight."

"Now you must decide what you shall perform," Xanthe informed them, and waved the pair to a far corner of the room before extending her silver bowl to Harriet Eavesly. That young lady found herself paired with Bertie Cumberland, who professed himself pleased as punch.

Daventry watched with interest as Xanthe next approached Charlotte Lynton. That lady displayed no hesitation, merely reaching in and withdrawing her partner's name. She read it, and a soft smile touched her lips.

"Captain Grayson," she announced.

Frederick? Now, what the devil was Xanthe about? he wondered. He had been certain—then he realized Desdemona Lynton had drawn a name, and now regarded him with a speculative gaze. Desdemona. He would be paired with that flighty, impulsive . . . a twinge of foreboding settled over him. It would take far more time and effort than he cared to spend to keep that young lady from entrapping him into playing some outrageous role.

She came to his side, a hint of laughter in her

eyes. "I know precisely which scene you will wish to enact," she informed him.

"Do you?" He eyed her warily.

"Of course. *Othello*. The scene where he smothers Desdemona."

A rumbling chuckle escaped him. "Appropriate," he agreed.

"Unless you would rather do the scene from *Hamlet* where he utterly casts off Ophelia and the poor girl goes mad."

"You'd enjoy playing a mad scene, I expect."

An impish grin answered that sally. "Oh, I'm no great actress. Or are you implying I would not have to act?"

He shook his head, smiling in turn. "I would have expected you to prefer the balcony scene from *Romeo and Juliet*."

"With that oak tree as the balcony, I suppose?" Then, in an unexpected rush of candor, she said, "I am terribly sorry about that incident. I do things without thinking, without considering the consequences, sometimes. Aunt Charlotte is forever telling me I must not be so impulsive, and I do try, but then something happens and I forget all my good intentions."

"But a most noble impulse," he said. Her apology charmed him, and the mixture of contrition and laughter in her lovely face tugged at him, at something locked deep within him he couldn't quite identify. So unfamiliar, so long disused, it took a few moments for him to recognize a reawakening sense of enjoyment, of a sudden longing to share her haphazard approach to life.

The corners of her mouth primmed as she tried to hold back a smile. "Since it is Yule, do you not think we should do something from *A Midsummer Night's Dream?*"

"You shall have to play Puck," he responded at once, the gaiety of her mood infecting him.

She wrinkled her nose. "You would do it so much better."

"Whatever makes you think such an outlandish thing?" he demanded, taken aback. Yet to his horror, he found the playful role appealed to him.

He turned away, appalled, not wanting her to see his confusion. To be enthusiastic, haphazard, to let one's curiosity drive one as Miss Lynton did—no, it wasn't to be thought of. She cast a dizzying spell, infecting him with her irresponsibility. His experiences had taught him the seriousness of command, and he saw many similarities between his current situation and the campaigns he had carried out in the past.

He had to remain responsible.

Five

Daventry sat at his desk, holding several sheets of paper on which his agent had painstakingly enumerated a lengthy list of repairs, costs, and estimates of the amount of time and workers each task would require. His thoughts, though, for once were not concentrated on the estate. He might stare at the papers, but his eyes saw not words, but Miss Desdemona Lynton's laughter-filled eyes and mischievous smile. A rare handful, that young lady, and one possessed of a singularly delightful air about her. In other circumstances . . .

No, not under any circumstances. The mere thought of that hey-go-mad child trying to run his home with any degree of comfort or order was absurd, and he was absurd to experience a tinge of regret. He had best return to his work, accomplish something in this rare hour of freedom before his houseguests returned from whatever expedition Xanthe had organized for their entertainment. Once they again infested his house, he would have his hands filled with playing the role of congenial host.

In his mind, he heard Desdemona Lynton's laugh

and her voice chiding him last night for being so rigid in his approach to acting. Well, that was his nature. He could do nothing about it, and he needed to return to his work.

He still sat at his desk, gazing abstractedly into space, reflecting on the musical quality of her voice, when a tap sounded on the door and William, the second footman, entered to announce the arrival of Mr. Doncaster and Mr. Beardsley. Vexed at himself for having wasted so much of his precious time, he set the papers aside and made his way to the salon, where the two clergymen again awaited him. *Will they make this a daily visit?* he wondered as he greeted first one and then the other.

Something of his irritation must have shown on his countenance, for Mr. Beardsley flashed an apologetic smile at him. "It seems we disturb you again," he said.

"Not in the least," Daventry proclaimed, gathering good breeding about him like armor. And there came the sound of carriages pulling up to the house. His solitude had indeed come to an end for that day.

The door flew open, and two men wearing knee-length surplices emblazoned with stars strode in. They raised yard-long brass instruments to their lips and blasted a fanfare. Visible notes cascaded from the bells of the horns, swirling about the room in a dance of carefree abandon, then drifting through the windowpanes to evaporate in the chill air of the late morning. Behind the musicians came a trio of nymphs, their long fair hair and misty drapery flowing, who scattered flower petals that exploded into cascades of multicolored sparks before hitting the floor. Then Xanthe strode in, followed closely by Lady Eugenia and her mother, Miss Eavesly, and Miss Charlotte Lynton, with Desdemona following behind.

The two clergymen rose to greet the new arrivals as the nymphs scurried to the side of the room. None of the others seemed aware of their presence—none, at least, except Desdemona. The girl's brow creased, and she glanced about the room as if she sensed some oddity, something she couldn't quite identify. Then Mr. Eavesly, accompanied by Sir Joshua and Lord Lowestoft, joined them, and her attention was claimed by her father.

The curate, who addressed Daventry, spoke in tones that carried throughout the room. "You have heard about Ramsgate Park and Willoughby House? No? Both broken into in the last three days. We only learned of it this morning."

"Terrible thing." Mr. Doncaster shook his shaggy gray head. "Terrible. And to have a Runner about the place! Not at all the sort of thing to which we are accustomed in this neighborhood."

"A Runner?" Desdemona looked up, her eyes gleaming as if the prospect fascinated her. "The very thing!"

"Desdi!" exclaimed her aunt in dismay. "No, you cannot—" She broke off, but fixed the girl with a forbidding look.

Cannot what? Daventry wondered. *Follow him around on his inquiries?* That sounded like the sort of thing Miss Desdemona Lynton would do.

"Matter needs looking into," declared Sir Joshua, interrupting Daventry's reflections. "Can't have these criminals stealing everything they can carry. Has this Runner fellow discovered who's responsible?"

"I cannot say," the rector declared sadly. "He only arrived yesterday—or was it the day before? Dear me, when was it? My dear Mr. Beardsley, do you recall which night we sat down to Mrs. Hargreave's excellent mutton? That's when Mr. Ramsgate called to tell us of the Runner's arrival. I remember it distinctly, for we were talking of the mint jelly, which reminded me of—" He broke off, his features growing puzzled. "It reminded me of something. Can't remember what, at the moment."

"He came this morning," Mr. Beardsley said gently. "And we came over here straightaway, because we thought Lord Daventry should be apprised of the situation and because it will naturally be of interest to Sir Joshua, as his home was one of those which has been robbed."

The rector fixed his curate with a confused gaze. "We had mutton for breakfast?"

Lady Eugenia shivered and took a step nearer Daventry, as if seeking his protection. "Oh, how I hope they apprehend these horrible men quickly. Why, what if they were to try to break in here while we were all asleep? We might be murdered in our beds!"

"Their method," explained Sir Joshua, "appears to be to strike when the families are from home. I believe we need not fear."

"Has no one seen anything that might help?" Desdemona demanded, looking about the room. "Surely someone, a stable hand or a footman, perhaps, must have glimpsed a cart, a horse, anything that might provide some clue as to their identities."

Mr. Beardsley shook his head. "If they have, they dare say nothing."

She turned her large, sparkling eyes on him. "Why ever not?"

The curate hesitated, then cast an apologetic glance at Charlotte Lynton. "Forgive me for mentioning it, but I have heard the men have threatened to kill anyone they catch spying on them."

Lady Eugenia emitted a squeak of alarm and moved even closer to Daventry.

"And have they?" the earl asked. "Killed anyone, I mean. I thought there had only been robberies."

"As far as I know," Mr. Beardsley said. "But the threat is being repeated in the villages around here. It makes it less likely anyone will be willing to assist this Bow Street Runner, this Mr. Pimm, who has come."

"It is all so dreadful," murmured Miss Charlotte Lynton.

Her face had paled, Daventry noted, and her expression was troubled.

"Irresponsible talk," declared Frederick. He moved to Miss Lynton's side, and his smile held a wealth of warmth and confidence. "These robbers probably started the rumors themselves, simply to keep anyone from trying to learn anything about them. Probably a pack of cowards. Undoubtedly, in fact. Do you not agree, Aubrey?"

"Assuredly." Daventry watched his cousin's ease and assurance with fascination. Well, she was a soothing young woman, not in the least terrifying. It would do Frederick a world of good to realize not all females looked upon him with pity or horror because of his missing arm. Miss Lynton obviously possessed the knack of putting him at his ease. That pleased Daventry. It seemed to him important that his countess—whoever she might be—should be able to put people at their ease.

Mr. Doncaster and Mr. Beardsley remained to partake of an elaborate nuncheon, then took their leave. Sir Joshua announced his intention to retire to the library for a nap, while the other gentlemen of the party decided to play billiards. Lady Eugenia, Miss Eavesly, and Miss Marcome declared their intentions to practice their instruments, and the other ladies chose to spend an hour or so pleasurably occupied over their needlework.

There might be a chance, Daventry mused, for him to slip into the estate office and join Mr. Charburton for a little while. Then he noticed the frown on Desdemona's face. He strolled over to her side, aware of the gleam in her large green eyes. "You are displeased with the schemes for this afternoon?" he inquired.

"No," she said slowly. "Except . . ." She trailed off.

"Except perhaps you would rather be outside again?"

Her countenance brightened. "Indeed. I don't

mean to be trouble, but staying within doors on such a crisp day does seem a trifle flat."

He considered. He had been wanting to ride out to where the repairs were being made to the great barn; he could use her desire to ride as an excuse. Or did he use the barn as an excuse to spend time with Desdemona? He rejected that thought and fixed a smile to his face. "Would you care to ride about the estate a little?"

She regarded him with that candid look in her eyes. Remarkably fine eyes, too, he noted, then chided himself for his whimsy. If he took her riding, it would be to please her aunt, not Desdemona.

Her brow wrinkled. *"You* want to ride," she accused him.

He gave up any attempt at pretense. "I admit I would be glad of the excuse to check on the progress of some work."

She considered for a moment, then nodded. "I will be ready in ten minutes." She turned on her heel and strode toward the door.

He would be surprised if he saw her again in less than half an hour. Resigned, he sent the message to the stable and made his way to his chamber to change from his morning coat. Yet when he returned to the salon some fifteen minutes later, now garbed in buckskins, riding boots, and a coat that had seen its share of campaigning, he was surprised to find her there before him.

She sprang to her feet as he opened the door. "You didn't believe I'd be ready, did you?" she asked gaily.

He inclined his head. "Let us say it is a delightful surprise."

He escorted her to the stable, where Laertes, a good-natured if somewhat fun-loving roan, stood saddled and waiting for her. She eyed the animal with interest, accepted Daventry's hand in tossing her into the saddle, then pulled aside her skirt to allow him to adjust her stirrup. By the time he had himself mounted Clumsy, the Roman-nosed chestnut who had accompanied him through most of the Peninsula, Desdemona was circling the yard, accustoming herself to her mount's mouth and temperament.

They set off side by side in a silence that crackled with tension. He could think of any number of things to say to break it, yet they all sounded inane in his mind. He would give a great deal to simply relax and enjoy his ride, yet how could he with her so close, swaying easily with her mount's gait, making him vividly aware of her, of the bright color whipped into her cheeks by the chill air, of the sparkle in her eyes at being outdoors and active?

Damn it, she was a mere chit of a girl. Determined to free his mind of this ludicrous obsession with her, he began a lecture about the estate, based mostly on what Mr. Charburton had taught him. As he continued, he became aware of a gleam growing in her eyes. He was handling her wrong, he knew, yet how the devil was one to deal with a chit whose mere presence unsettled him, made him want to drag her into his arms and kiss her just to experience the delight of her response? If only she were more responsible, more dependable, more unlike herself.

When they reached the barn, he did little more than subject it to a cursory scrutiny. The sooner he escaped from her company, the better it would be. Fixing his mind firmly on the highly instructive subjects of the crops and repairs, he brought them back to the stable.

She swung from her horse without waiting for help, then curtsied to him as if she were still in the schoolroom. "Thank you ever so much for the lesson, my lord," she said in a little girl's voice, then turned and skipped back to the house as if she were still a child.

Amusement vied with his sudden embarrassment and won. Lord, she'd called him to book right enough. He'd been preachy and boring, and so she'd let him know in no uncertain terms. The devil of it was, it made him appreciate her all the more.

He had not finished with her that day, either. Xanthe decreed that the evening must be spent in rehearsing their various skits, and he found himself relegated to a far corner of the Ivory Drawing Room with Desdemona his sole companion. She perched on the edge of her chair, a copy of *A Midsummer Night's Dream* open on her lap, a slight frown creasing her brow as she studied the play. At last she set it down in disgust. "I can find very little where two people are alone!"

"We could choose something different," he suggested.

She eyed him coldly. "Very well, *Othello* it is. You may have the pleasure of smothering me." She left him, only to return shortly with the other play, flipping through its pages. "Where is that scene?"

"Here." He took it from her, his hand brushing hers as he did so. It took a moment to return his thoughts to Shakespeare. After a brief search, he handed it back.

She perused it, then frowned again. "As much as I feel certain you would take great joy in the murdering, I cannot feel the scene is suitable."

He read it. "No," he agreed at last.

She sighed. "Then we shall have to do the balcony scene from *Romeo and Juliet.*"

He looked up, appalled.

"Only we shall play it as a comedy," she finished.

"With you hanging in a tree?" he asked before he could stop himself. To his consternation, a delightful blush flooded her cheeks.

She lowered her face into her hands and her shoulders trembled. After a moment, she said in a shaking voice, "Is—is it not time we forget that incident?"

"My dear Miss Lynton." He leaned forward, just touching her hand. "I do beg your pardon. It was unforgivable of me—"

"Quite right." She looked up, grinning, her eyes dancing. "And let that be a lesson to you."

He sat back. "Baggage," he said with considerable feeling.

She mimed a curtsy, then sprang to her feet. "I'll bring another play."

He watched her hurry from the room, her steps light, almost dancing. Dancing. There would be a ball the following night, one of Xanthe's devising. He very much looked forward to seeing Desdemona taking part in a set, moving to the music. Despite her childlike sense of fun, there was little of the child about her.

Perhaps he'd been wrong to hold her at a distance. Every minute he spent in her company, he became more and more aware of her as a desirable young woman. Perhaps—but he had no intention of progressing quickly, not with the importance of the choice he must make. Still, he found himself thinking of the next night with pleasurable anticipation.

That mood lasted him through dinner the following evening, but not much longer after that. A ball, he decided, had to be the hardest of all facets of polite society to which he must adjust. He heartily wished himself locked in his estate office, planning his campaign against neglect with military precision. That was the life for him, not this social whirl of entertaining and being surrounded by people who could talk of nothing but other entertainments. He could imagine nothing more different from his familiar routine in the military.

He shifted his position, aware that the formal ball dress did not suit him nearly as well as did a uniform. He felt uncomfortable, out of his depth as he stood at the door to the great hall, watching the silk- and satin-gowned ladies with their jewels glimmering in the candlelight. The other gentlemen, elegant in their finest coats, appeared calm and assured in these surroundings. Why could he not be like them?

As for his house, he hardly recognized it. Xanthe

had given the servants a magical hand, of course. Nothing else could explain the fantastic transformation of the ballroom into a garden of holly and white roses. The blossoms filled every conceivable space, their heady scent heavy in the air.

Xanthe herself wore a white silk robe with an apron of blond lace, and a matching spray of roses and ostrich plumes woven through her thick, fair hair. She stood at his side, guiding him through the social niceties that had never before come in his way. Behind them, the orchestra—all garbed in white—warmed up. A flute ran liltingly up a scale, a violin answered, and a cello filled in with a deeper note. Daventry fought back a surge of panic.

"You will do very well," Xanthe murmured for his ear alone.

"I haven't danced in more than eleven years," he hissed back.

"Tonight," she assured him with that smile that just failed to be prim, "you will put the others to shame."

"I'll settle for not disgracing myself," he shot back, then greeted Sir Roland and Lady Ashborough as the majordomo announced their names.

He had first to lead out the countess of Lowestoft, who took the opportunity to assure him he would find more pleasure in dancing with her daughter. "Impossible," Daventry responded, then realized that, while flattering, this was not the response that lady wished to hear.

"A delightful girl, is she not?" pursued that determined parent. "We have lavished the greatest care on her upbringing. Such accomplishments! Such beauty. We are quite proud of her. She may look as high as she wishes for a match, though you may be sure she would not despise equaling the rank of her mamma."

For a moment, he thought wistfully of giving such blatant matchmaking the set-down it deserved, but with an effort restrained himself. Matchmaking was, after all, the purpose of this whole round of entertainments. And the countess spoke no more than the truth. Lady Eugenia possessed beauty and manners to please the most exacting gentleman. And she did please him, to an extent. Only he wanted more than capability in his wife.

That surprised him. He would have sworn he would marry the first practical female to cross his path. Now that he had a houseful of such admirable young ladies from which to choose, he found he wanted more.

As he circled his partner in the movements of the dance, he sought out each of the young ladies selected by Xanthe for his inspection. There was Harriet Eavesly in pink gauze and pearls, her fair hair clustered in becoming ringlets. Fanny Marcome, all in pale blue silk with her dark hair falling to her shoulders from a jeweled knot at the crown of her head, danced with the elegant if dandified Lord Lowestoft. Mr. Beardsley had won the honor of leading out Lady Eugenia, breathtaking in yellow and amber, all raven curls and flashing blue eyes. Charlotte Lynton stood beside her brother, laughing, proclaiming her assurance and independence in azure satin with a necklet of diamonds and sapphires.

And then there was Desdemona. He couldn't help but smile as he caught a glimpse of her as she curtsied to young Mr. Eavesly. Daventry bowed as required by the dance, but his thoughts remained on the laughing girl in the peach-colored silk with a strip of blond lace in the decolletage. She seemed perpetually in motion, every bit as graceful as he'd expected. She floated through the movements as if she were part of the music.

To his consternation, he found himself following her with his gaze over the next several country dances. He knew he owed it solely to Xanthe's assistance that he performed his own part with any degree of credit. He might concentrate for a short while on his current partner, but Desdemona's laugh, or even a passage in the music, made him think of her once more, and he'd scan the room until he found her.

She promenaded with Mr. Beardsley at the moment, the curate sporting a surprisingly elegant toe. His expression betokened a serious turn of conversation between them. Then the movement of the dance brought her into clearer view, and he could see her eagerness, her intensity. They probably discussed the housebreakings, he reflected. He'd heard more than one uneasy conversation concerning this distressing topic of whether any of the guests might return home to find they had become the next victims.

That fear might have cast a pall over the evening,

but no clouds of concern hovered long over the revelers. For that, he suspected he again had Xanthe to thank. Because of her magical intervention, gaiety filled the room. Candles flickered with more than normal brightness. The champagne bubbled in the glasses with unusual zest. Platters of refreshments looked incredibly appetizing, their aromas tantalizing the senses. Even the music surged through him with compelling delight. He'd have to have a talk with his fairy godmother about overdoing it. If he weren't careful, he'd get caught up in this magical night.

The music drew to a close, and he escorted his current partner, Lady Eugenia, back to Lady Lowestoft, then turned to fulfill another obligation. Only he didn't want to. He wanted to enjoy himself, laugh for the sheer pleasure of laughing, feel his cares and worries and obligations melt away from him. He wanted to dance with Desdemona.

A delighted peal of laughter rang out, and his heart quickened. He turned toward the source, and there she stood, just beyond the next knot of people, squeezing her aunt's hands in some playful jest. Ridiculous chit, all fun loving, no sense of duty. Yet at the moment, he didn't care. He wasn't making a lifelong commitment to her, after all. He merely sought her hand for the set that formed.

As he started toward them, Frederick approached from the other side. "May I beg you to sit out this next dance with me?" he inquired of Miss Charlotte Lynton.

"I should be delighted," she informed him, a gentle contrast to her lively niece. "But do, pray, let us get some punch first, for I am dying of thirst."

Frederick offered her his arm, then cast a quizzical glance at Daventry as the earl strolled up to join them. "Have I stolen a march on you?"

"Miss Lynton has already honored me," he assured his cousin. "I have come to see if Miss Desdemona will risk herself."

The girl's eyebrows rose. "Don't you mean it will be *you* who risk yourself?" she inquired.

"I have faced armies in battle," he assured her as he led her to where a set formed. "Dancing with you is not likely to prove more hazardous."

"True," she agreed as she took his hand for the first movement. "I can hardly fall out of anything onto you at the moment."

His shoulders shook with his deep chuckle. No, there would be no harm in dancing with the chit, he reflected as she circled him, her impish gaze never leaving his. She lifted his spirits, which had sunk to low ebb with this shift in his life, with the giving up of all he had known for the past eleven years. She might not be suitable for the role of his wife, but perhaps she could be a friend.

He extended his left arm behind her to take her left hand, his other clasping her right before them as they began the promenade. Her shoulder pressed against his chest and the top of her curls brushed against his mouth. They smelled of roses and violets and springtime, and suddenly he wanted to sweep her into his arms and kiss her, see if she tasted of strawberries and cream.

Damn Xanthe, he swore inwardly. Her magic worked at the wrong moment, when he danced with the wrong lady. And why must they wear gloves? He would much rather be holding her hand without the supple leather between them. He certainly didn't want to release her as required by the movement, but he did, and forced himself to look straight ahead as she circled him once more, rather than allowing his gaze to follow her every light step, her every provocative, swaying movement. Her curls bounced—not much, just enough to make him aware of them, of her.

She wasn't the right lady to be his wife. His militarily pragmatic side knew this, set off claxons and alarums in his mind, warned him he must not indulge this dangerous whim. He could do nothing that might raise her expectations. He could not, must not, offer for her. He needed a practical, sensible wife, not some giddy child who would sweep him off into larks and games. He needed a helpmate to be lady of the manor, to carry soup to ailing tenants, to assist the rector with his concerns in the parish. He needed a worldly wise chaperon to guide his sisters through the pitfalls of their coming London Seasons. Yet with every passing moment, it became harder to heed such practical counsel.

He wanted Desdemona, and a long-buried reckless streak stirred within him, whispering to let practical matters be damned.

Six

Desdi stood at her aunt's side, her gaze following Daventry as he set forth to find his next partner. Whoever the lucky woman might be, she couldn't possibly have a more wonderful time with him than Desdi had. If only she could dance with him again and again and again. . . .

"He is a very amiable man," remarked Aunt Charlotte with real sincerity of feeling.

Desdi's lips twitched. "I wouldn't call him amiable, precisely." Fascinating, definitely. Stubborn and autocratic, without a doubt. Commanding and mesmerizing and wholly enthralling, absolutely. But amiable?

Charlotte regarded her with a puzzled frown. "I quite thought you liked Captain Grayson. He certainly spends much of his time with you and his cousin's half sisters."

"Oh!" Desdi felt herself flushing. "I thought you meant—" She broke off, but her gaze strayed to where the earl stood, momentarily trapped between Lady Lowestoft and her daughter.

"Daventry?" Aunt Charlotte tilted her fair head to

one side, considering. "He has certainly shown us every kindness, and I know from Mr. Doncaster he is proving to be a generous landlord. I believe that slight reserve of his comes from his being so long away from home with the army. Once he grows more accustomed to our country life, I feel certain he shall be as amiable as one could wish."

He already was everything she could wish, Desdi reflected. Everything, that was, except one thing: He was not in love with her.

For a few moments while they'd danced, she'd thought him on the verge of swinging her, laughing, into his arms. But he hadn't, of course. It had emanated from her own wistful imaginings.

Aside from how shockingly improper such a course of conduct would have been, he seemed more inclined to hold her at the length of those same strong arms. As she lay awake in her bed at night, she remembered how it felt when he'd caught her as she'd fallen from that ridiculous tree, how her heart had pounded, how she'd been aware of nothing but the brilliance of his hazel eyes, the rough stubble of growth on his cheek, the scent of old leather that clung to him.

No, she couldn't deny the strength of her attraction, those tantalizing tugs at her heart that betokened a *tendre* of no mean order. In fact, if she did not cut it short at once, it might well turn to love. However wonderful that thought might be, she was far too aware that her impulsive nature made her unsuitable for the role of a countess. Why, oh why, could her heart and head not agree? Her longing for him left her aching inside.

"Has something distressed you?" a gentle voice asked.

She looked up to see Mr. Beardsley standing at her side. She shook her head and managed a bright smile. "It is merely growing quite late for me. I must be a bird at heart, for I wake with the dawn and grow weary soon after the sun sets. I should have sought my perch long ago."

"Then you have much in common with our good rector." Mr. Beardsley nodded in the direction of the chairs that lined the wall. In one, very near the table that held the punch bowl and champagne bottles, sat the elderly Mr. Doncaster, his head bowed forward so his chin rested on his broad chest. His head jerked slightly, then settled once more, but if he snored, Desdi could not hear it over the strains of the orchestra and the babble of conversations.

"He does not look comfortable," Desdi said. "Should you not take him home?"

"It would be best," he agreed. Yet he hesitated, making no move to do so.

Desdi eyed him with speculation. He was a youngish man, probably not yet thirty, with a suppressed energy that must come in useful in a parish this size. Yet that would be work; even if his heart lay deeply with the people he helped shepherd, he probably longed for a little amusement.

He shook his head, met her gaze, and a touch of ruefulness crept over his features. "Would you mind watching him, just to make certain he does not fall? I will find Lady Xanthe and make our excuses."

Desdi smiled after his departing figure, then made her way to the side of the snoozing rector. He looked so very peaceful. It would be a shame to wake him and take him out into the cold night.

As she studied him, his eyes opened and his gaze came to rest directly on her. "Miss Lynton," he pronounced, and smiled. "If I were but twenty years younger, I should ask for your hand for the next dance. But I am not." He fell asleep again.

The two gentlemen from the rectory departed some twenty minutes later, with the old man wrapped warmly in blankets against the elements and with a hot brick at his feet. Desdi, who had followed them to the door, wished them both a cheery good night, then made her way back to the ballroom. There she found George Eavesly waiting to take her in to supper. As soon as they had finished, a local youth claimed her for the next dance. Bertie Cumberland led her out after that, and by the time they left the floor, she could no longer stifle her yawns. She said her good nights, her thoughts already upstairs occupying her warm, comfortable bed.

She had one more task to complete before she could seek it, though. She browsed through the refreshments table, selecting a variety of delicacies that would keep until the following day, then stumbled sleepily up the stairs to the schoolroom suite, where Bella and Sophie slumbered in their respective beds in spite of their determination to remain awake to watch the last of the guests depart. The remains of an earlier treat, which she had sent up with Robert before the supper, lay on a low table. Smiling, Desdi whispered an unheard good night, placed the tray where the girls would be sure to find it, then made her way along the corridors until she came at last to her own chamber.

Once she was between sheets, though, her drowsiness vanished. She lay awake long, restless, treasuring the memory of Daventry's every touch and glance. If she closed her eyes very tight, she could see his face, study each angle and plane, each expression she had begun to know so well. In short, she could behave like a lovesick fool. She rolled over and concentrated on reciting various snatches of poetry, studiously memorized but long abandoned, which became more and more ludicrous as sleep crept over her.

She awoke at her usual early hour somewhat bleary-eyed and out of sorts. Casting back the draperies at her window, she stared moodily across the back garden toward the fields beyond. A light dusting of snow covered the ground and clung to the branches and shrubs. What she needed, she decided, was a long gallop to clear the fog from her mind and the depression from her spirits. If she could bear the escort of one of Daventry's grooms, it might be possible.

She scrambled into her riding habit, and fifteen minutes later she reached the bottom of the great stair and started across the tiled entry hall. As she paused to consider which exit would bring her closest to her desired destination, Daventry emerged from the servants' wing dressed in the same military coat, buckskins, and boots he'd worn the other afternoon when they rode. In one hand he carried a large slab of bread; in the other he held a tankard.

He stopped, raising his eyebrows. "You are about early this day. I would have thought you'd need to sleep late to recover."

"I can never stay abed in the morning," she told him with mock sorrow. "No matter how late I go to sleep, I am awake at the same hour."

"Sounds beastly uncomfortable," he said.

She laughed. "I suppose you have the soldier's habit of being able to sleep anytime you have a spare five minutes."

"I seem to be losing it," he admitted.

"And to think you have been a civilian for less than two months." She shook her head sadly. "But you have retained the soldier's ability to find a meal." She regarded him hopefully.

He led her along the maze of passages to the kitchens, where a giggling maid was induced to cut another slab of cheese and the bread fresh from the oven. Thus armed, they set forth for the stables. As they walked through the chill, yew-scented air, Desdi cast a sideways glance at the man striding briskly at her side. She could think of no one she would rather spend time with. Had she been right last night that he'd looked at her with a warmth that was absent when his gaze rested on other ladies? Even on Aunt Charlotte? She cradled the hope close to her, afraid to let it out for fear it might break.

* * *

Daventry reined in at the top of a low rise. The chill breeze stung his face and ruffled the hair about his ears. He drew a deep breath, savoring the crisp, clean air that filled his lungs. He hadn't felt so exhilarated since just before his last battle as he rode the line of his men, shouting encouragement, exchanging jokes, heedless of risk, and living for that moment alone.

From slightly behind him, Desdi let out a sigh of sheer pleasure. "That," she remarked as she eased her blowing mount to his side, "was a thoroughly enjoyable race."

His gaze rested on her, on her face glowing pink from exposure to the wind, on her eyes that sparkled with youth and vigor, on her parted lips. Her intriguing bosom rose and fell with the quickness of her breathing. He'd never seen her more lovely, not even in her ball gown with—

Ball gown. Ball. Guests. Responsibilities.

The thoughts jolted back into his mind, which had been so wonderfully free of worry for the last half hour and more. He had intended to escape for no longer than that, to be back at the house by now to greet the earliest of the risers as they made their way down to the breakfast parlor in search of the fragrant coffee and cinnamon buns that wafted their aromas throughout the rambling old building.

"We won't be missed yet," Desdi said, as if she had read his mind.

He realized he stared back the way they had

come, and felt the frown that creased his brow. His feelings must have been obvious, and that annoyed him.

"No one is likely to venture out until at least noon," she added.

A sudden smile tugged at his lips. "You did," he pointed out.

"Yes, and like the excellent host you are, you have seen to my morning's entertainment. You may continue to do so, and you will have a clear conscience."

It tempted him, but he shook his head. "Others may well be about by now. We should not have come so far."

"You may lay the blame on me." She turned Laertes, and the neat little roan picked his dainty way along the path through the winter grass, down to the cart track below. She glanced over her shoulder to where he followed, the laughter still in her bright eyes. "Say my ferocious mount bolted with me, and it was miles before you were able to overtake us and bring me to safety. You will be quite the hero for all the ladies."

He regarded her with as much disapproval as he could muster. "That won't be necessary." Still, the idea of rescuing her appealed to him, though he had a strong suspicion she could handle anything as mundane as a runaway horse.

When they reached the house at last, Desdi went at once to her room to change her dress. Daventry would have liked to do the same, but he made his way first to the breakfast parlor to see if his lapse as host had gone undetected. It had not. He found Sir Joshua, Lord Lowestoft, and Bertie Cumberland in the sunny chamber, with the remnants of substantial meals on their plates. Sir Joshua lounged back in his chair, a tankard of homebrew in his hand, his expression one of benevolent contentment. He greeted Daventry with a wave, then addressed himself to the plate of buns that sat before him.

"It seems I must apologize for being absent." Daventry remained by the door, conscious of his betraying garments with their clinging horsehairs and splattering of mud.

Bertie Cumberland raised his quizzing glass and leveled it at him. "Out so early?" He stifled a yawn.

"Military men." Lord Lowestoft shook his head, as if in lack of comprehension of this breed.

"You and my daughter," said Sir Joshua, with his indulgent parental smile. "Always up and doing at first light. Surprised you didn't run into her."

"I did," Daventry admitted. "She is changing at the moment, which is what I must do." He excused himself and exited the room, very much aware of Sir Joshua's startled and speculative gaze fastened on his back.

As he reached the stairs and put his hand on the balustrade, Mrs. Seymour, the new housekeeper, emerged from the nether regions of the hall and made her purposeful way toward him. It seemed he was not yet to put off his dirt. He waited for her, and she stopped several yards from him, her hands clasped before her, her pointed chin jutted out.

She cleared her throat. "My lord, I fear I must

bring tidings to you of dreadful mismanagement. There is not a sheet in the cupboards that is not in need of darning. There are no preserves in the pantry. No, nor any remedies laid up against this wet season. The maids are lax in their duties, and I do not see how this household has managed with so few. Why, Colonel Marcome had to ring four times before one of the girls went to see what was needed. And as for the kitchens! My lord, they are a disgrace, what with the chipped crockery—"

His jaw tightened and he held up his hand. He really didn't want this reminder of his neglected duties to his guests. "Make a list of everything that needs attention and give it to Mr. Charburton. I will see to it at once." He turned and finally mounted the stairs.

Such complaints should be taken to the mistress of the household, not to him. A pang of guilt struck him that he should bring some poor unfortunate female into an establishment as ill-run as this. What the devil of a lot of work she would have on her hands bringing everything into order. She would have help, of course, from the majordomo and housekeeper, but it took more than an efficient staff to assure guests were made comfortable and welcome. It took a capable mistress of the establishment.

Into his mind erupted the image of Desdi, laughing, mischievous, careless of the conventions. An answering spark stirred within him, then faded. She was nothing more than a child. She would be completely incapable of dealing with the problems his household presented.

She would grow older, he reminded himself. She would learn what was needed from her.

But she wouldn't change. She would remain haphazard and fun-loving, and he had a terrible, sinking feeling she might shirk the duties she found distasteful.

How might she respond to discovering she must act as chaperon to a couple of schoolroom misses straining at their tethers to make their debuts to society? What could a chit her age really know of the dangers and pitfalls lurking in a London Season? No, his half sisters needed a mature and provident guide through the social maze more than he needed a laughing child who set his desires aflame.

Troubled, he reached the top stair to find a miniature form of Xanthe hovering at the level of his shoulder, her legs curled under her so she sat on the air as if it were a cushion. Her chin rested in one hand, and as he paused to stare at her, she shook her head in exaggerated sorrow.

"Look at yourself," she declared, and hummed a soft bar.

A hand mirror appeared before him, and he stared into his haggard reflection. A deep furrow carved his brow, the line of his jaw strained with tension, and his expression could only be described as grim.

"Men can be so foolish," Xanthe declared.

"I had always thought us to be practical creatures." Something pressed against his leg, and he leaned down to stroke the immense white form of Titus.

"Foolish," Xanthe repeated, her tone brooking no argument.

"What the devil do you expect me to do?" he demanded.

"Follow your heart's desire," came her prompt response.

He drew in an exasperated breath. "Do you think I'm not trying? I don't suppose you could have made it simpler?"

"My dear boy, there are limits to what I can—and should—do for you."

He regarded her with growing irritation. "You made it sound as if you could do anything."

Her eyes glittered. "I could turn you into a frog, but would that be good for you?"

He felt his color darken. "I beg your pardon."

She laughed suddenly, her aura of mischief returning. "Poor Aubrey, but you must understand. I *could* grant you the wish of your heart, present it to you on a platter, as it were. But would you recognize it?"

He blinked. "I—" He broke off, disturbed by this new thought.

"You would not," she went on softly. "You don't yet know what you want most in your heart of hearts. If I simply came out and told you, you wouldn't appreciate it. You wouldn't know what it meant to you. You must decide for yourself how best to manage your life. You must make your own choices and know, in your heart, they are the right ones."

His lips twitched in reluctant amusement. "You couldn't see your way to giving me a few hints?"

Amusement sparkled about her, taking the form of tiny flares of brilliant color. "I have provided you with the opportunity to discover it, to grasp what you most want. But you must make the move. You must reach out to capture it."

She vanished.

A *myap* came from near the floor, and Daventry looked down at Titus, who stared reproachfully at the empty space where the tiny fairy form of Xanthe had been. A rounded, gold-tipped feather lay on the carpet at his feet. "She likes to be exasperating, doesn't she?" he asked.

Titus blinked sleepy green eyes at him. The tip of his tail twitched; then the cat turned about and sauntered off.

"And she's not the only one," Daventry muttered, and continued on to his chamber to change into more suitable garments.

He at last returned to the breakfast parlor to see how his guests got on, and found the newest arrivals partaking of a barely adequate meal. The housekeeper—or whoever approved the menus—should have ordered more dishes, and larger portions of each. At least his butler knew his job, for the silver gleamed and the ale flowed freely. The linen on the table showed a patch of darning, though, and should not have been used.

As the day progressed, more signs of his household's mismanagement assailed him. Nuncheon arrived late, and the menu appeared to have been selected at random, making use of whatever foods lay at hand in the pantry. Only the wine, brought up from the reserve laid down by his grandfather, raised the meal above the commonplace. He would have to speak to Mrs. Seymour. And why the devil didn't Xanthe see to it?

Because she only provided opportunities, not solutions. And possibly because he needed to learn that houses didn't simply run themselves, but needed a capable female at the helm.

In the early afternoon, the snow began to fall once more, lightly at first, then with a steadiness that offered no hope of an early relief. Half-formed plans of a riding expedition were abandoned, and the ladies retired to the music room to practice upon the pianoforte or harp, to embroider, or to sketch one another in those various occupations. With a sense of relief, Daventry escorted the gentlemen to the masculine sanctuary of the billiards room, where the lack of a feminine touch made no difference.

Still, and try as he might, he could not put the problem from his mind, and the fact that it remained a troubling problem should prove answer enough for him. As the earl of Daventry, he had certain obligations, to his name, to his tenantry, to his neighborhood. This included throwing his house open to weeklong parties, fetes, festivals, and a wide variety of other entertainments. He could not pretend— could not hope. He must be practical. That ridiculous ambition of his to capture Desdi in his arms, along with all the delightful possibilities he could try once he had her there, he must abandon.

He watched Lord Lowestoft take a careful shot without really seeing it. If he must saddle himself with a practical female . . . Mentally, he conjured up the image of each of his marriageable guests, rejecting them one after the other. Only one, only Charlotte Lynton, did not send a twinge of revulsion through him at the prospect of facing her across the breakfast table every morning for the rest of his life. He liked Miss Lynton. He didn't love her, of course, but one did not look for the passionate emotions in a marriage of convenience. Comfort and tolerable companionship would suffice. Once he had wed the capable young woman and seen the improvements in his home, his ill-judged infatuation with her niece would fade.

He fought back a sensation of bleakness. He was being foolish beyond permission. He would be quite content with Miss Lynton.

The door swung open, and Desdi herself blew in with a swirl of snow falling from her caped shoulders, her eyes sparkling, her cheeks shining with the cold and dampness that clung to her fair skin. His carefully and painfully reached decision fell apart.

Seven

Desdi hesitated on the threshold of the billiards room, glancing about the assembled company, the flakes on her hood melting so the drops ran down to her shoulders. "My lord!" she cried, a trifle breathless.

Daventry could only stare at her, mesmerized by the picture of youth and energy she presented, at everything upon which he must turn his back when he'd offered for her aunt.

Sir Joshua, who had been aiming his cue, straightened and thudded the end of the stick to the floor. "What do you mean, barging in like that, m'girl? Put a fellow off his shot."

She glanced at him. "Oh, I do beg your pardon, Pappa, but there are men outside!"

"Men?" Daventry pulled himself together. "What do you mean? Visitors?"

"I doubt you would encourage their sort," Desdi said with a sudden touch of humor. "It has grown quite dark, but I could just make them out, creeping about the grounds in a suspiciously stealthy manner. I thought you ought to know."

"Poachers?" suggested Frederick. He straightened from where he had been leaning against the wall beside Bertie Cumberland, watching the progress of the game.

Desdi shook her head. "I hadn't gone far from the house, and—"

"What were you doing outside in the first place?" demanded her pappa.

"I wanted exercise."

"Dash it, girl, it's snowing!" Sir Joshua protested, eyeing his daughter with marked disapproval.

"Which is why I was heading for the shrubbery, which looked sheltered," she explained. "But before—"

Sir Joshua shook his head. "Shoes will be damp. You know how your aunt will scold if you don't take them off right away."

"Yes, Pappa. Only I do think Lord Daventry should hear about those men." She turned back to him. "They were near the west wing, and I distinctly remember Bella telling me it is unoccupied, which means anyone might creep about there, or perhaps even force an entry, and there would be no one to hear."

"Good God." Lord Lowestoft's complexion paled. "Do you think she saw those damned housebreakers?"

"It seems unlikely," Daventry said, but found he didn't believe his reassurance.

"What, scouting about while it's still light?" Sir Joshua raised skeptical eyebrows.

"It's dusk," George Eavesly pointed out, excitement lighting his eyes.

"We'll have a look about, I think," Daventry decided, and pulled the bell to summon Finley.

"If you want to discover anything, you had best hurry," Desdi urged.

He glanced over his shoulder at her. "Are those men still there?"

"No, but—"

"Then we have time to summon aid for a thorough search."

In very short order, the footmen, armed with lanterns, set forth to scour the grounds. The grooms, roused from their cozy quarters above the stables, aided them. Not to be left out, the gentlemen of the house party donned their greatcoats and flocked outdoors, led by Desdi, to personally reassure themselves no nefarious rogues had skulked about the west wing.

They trooped across the lawn and the gravel paths leading into the rose garden in rare high spirits, despite the icy chill of the evening air. They thought it a lark, Daventry reflected. But what if Desdi were right? What if housebreakers *did* lurk behind every tree, threatening his home? What if—

Eavesly's excited exclamation broke across his thoughts. The young gentleman had hurried ahead, dragging Desdi with him, but she had stopped him, holding him back as she pointed toward the shrubbery bed beneath a low window.

"There's been someone here!" Eavesly called back over his shoulder. His eyes glittered with excitement in the wavering light from the lantern that swung in his hand. "See? Here, in this patch of fresh snow. Footprints!"

Sir Joshua peered over his shoulder. "A good number of them," he mused. "Trampled that patch over there, too."

Daventry studied the indicated areas, where heavy booted feet had ground the dusting of snow into the rich soil, creating a muddied slush.

The window above stood at a height of five feet; the earl tested it. To his consternation it shifted, moving an inch. "The devil," he muttered.

Lord Lowestoft peered at it through his quizzing glass. "Faulty latch, dear boy. Best have it looked to."

"Not so much faulty as pried." Daventry indicated the scratches, visible even by the light of the lantern.

Desdi shivered. "Do you think they meant to enter now, or were merely preparing their way for later tonight?"

Daventry turned his thoughtful gaze on her. "No one would have heard them, whenever they chose to come. I believe I must thank you for frightening them off. Did they see you, do you think?"

She shook her head. "Not to recognize me again, if that is what you mean. I certainly would not be able to identify them. But I do know where they went."

Her father stared at her, blinking. "The devil you do! How would you know a thing like that, miss?"

"I followed as far as I could before I lost their tracks in the darkness. The last I could tell, they were heading through the outbuildings of the home farm."

"What did you mean by following them?" Daventry demanded.

"Exactly my point," nodded Sir Joshua. "What if they'd turned on you?"

"I wasn't that close. If I had been, I might have learned something of some use. As it is, we know only a direction, and even that might not help us very much."

"We'll see where it leads as soon as it is light," Daventry decided.

"Light?" cried Desdi. "Why not now? We have lanterns, which I did not. We should be able to find their tracks in the snow."

"Theirs, and the grooms', and those of every other person who has passed through here since the last snow fell. Without daylight, we'd never be able to tell one set of footprints from another. No, it will have to wait until morning."

Desdi's chin thrust out. "But—"

"And you look quite chilled enough for one night," he snapped, interrupting her. "Frederick, take her back to the house, will you? We'll be along in a moment."

"But—" Desdi began again.

"Quite right," her father declared. "Can't have you taking a chill. Run along, m'girl. Go and find your aunt Charlotte. She'll know what's best to do for you."

"We might as well all return," said Frederick.

"Miss Lynton, will you not take my arm? The footing is treacherous."

She opened her mouth, but the kindness of his tone seemed to have a soothing effect on her. She accepted his cousin's assistance, which Daventry doubted she needed, and the two led the others back. The silly chit must be devilishly cold with only that cloak about her. He'd be glad of a fire himself.

They reentered the house by the front door, which was the nearest, to be met by Xanthe and the other ladies of the party, who stood grouped in the main hall, huddled in their shawls. "I rang for a footman, and instead got a very frightened maid wailing about our all being murdered in our beds," Xanthe explained.

"I saw them!" Desdi informed her. "The housebreakers."

"Desdi!" Alarm filled her aunt Charlotte's face. "My love—"

"I was quite some distance away," the young lady said with a noticeable touch of regret. "And I must say," she added, her bright eyes kindling once more, "had I known how poor spirited everyone would be, I should not have wasted my time coming back here to warn everyone, but followed them a great deal further than I did."

"Followed them?" gasped Charlotte. *"Further?"*

"I saw which way they went," Desdi insisted. "And I still say it would not be difficult to trace them, even now."

"No!" The word exploded from Daventry. "Good God, would you run headlong into danger? Have you no sense?" He saw the mutinous gleam in her eyes, and threw caution—or perhaps prudence—to the winds. "I absolutely forbid you to go outside alone after dark from now on. No." He held up his hand, silencing her outraged protest. "This is not open to discussion." He turned to her father. "I am sorry if this displeases you, Sir Joshua."

"Not in the least." Her doting pappa nodded his approval. "Enterprising little thing. Never know what mischief she'll be getting into next. Much better have her safe within doors if there's any danger lurking. Like as not, she'd walk right up to the villains and demand to know what they think they're about."

"Pappa!" The color burned bright in Desdi's cheeks.

"No, my love." Charlotte Lynton laid a restraining hand on her shoulder. "They are quite right, you know. We have no way of determining what those dreadful men might do. Leave this matter in the hands of the gentlemen. Depend upon it, my love, They will know what to do far better than we."

Desdi opened her mouth, shut it with a snap, then gave in to the torrent of words she could not contain. "Of all the poor spirited things to say! No, really, Aunt Charlotte, what makes *gentlemen* any better suited than we? We are being robbed every bit as much as they, and—"

"That's enough, m'girl," said Sir Joshua.

To Daventry's surprise, Desdi closed her mouth. Her expression spoke volumes, though, and if her doting pappa believed himself to have had the last word on the subject, Daventry doubted it. Not all comments needed to be spoken aloud.

"Come, my dear." Charlotte Lynton laid a hand on her niece's shoulder. "It will truly be the wisest course for us all to remain indoors once it has started to grow dark. It is much too cold at this season to be engaged upon any lark outside. And at the moment, I need your help with my costume for the skit we are giving. Will you not give me your advice?"

Desdi went with her aunt, but the look she cast over her shoulder at Daventry made it clear she was not being diverted. He watched them head up the stairs, aware of how very different they were from one another: Desdi all life and laughter, her aunt all calm good sense and gentle persuasion.

Charlotte Lynton would handle his half sisters with that same delicate touch, guiding their behavior with her sound judgment. She was, in short, eminently suitable for the position of his wife. He had best offer for her before he allowed Desdi's intoxicating liveliness to distract him from his sensible purpose again.

The first light woke Desdi, for she had been waiting for it. She might have been ordered to remain within doors at night, but it was no longer night. They could no longer use the excuse of darkness to delay the search that should have been made the night before.

She wanted to see Daventry, too, to see if his annoyance with her still lingered. She didn't like his coldness, the sensation he had shut a door between them and desired to keep her inextricably on the other side. He had maintained that attitude throughout the evening, avoiding her when he could, refusing to be drawn into a conversation when he could not. He had even gone so far as to excuse himself from rehearsing their scene for Christmas Eve, and the need to practice their parts grew urgent.

Well, as soon as she saw him this morning, she would place herself before him, where he could not ignore her. And then . . . well, inspiration would undoubtedly strike. She slipped from her bed into the chill air, decided with regret she would not remain in her chamber long enough to justify the lighting of a fire, and hurried into her riding habit.

As she descended the stairs, the deep, steady sound of Daventry's voice reached her, answered by a cheerful tenor in accents suggesting the back streets of London. "Can't escape us for much longer, m'lord. The great houses that've been hit—there's been a pattern to 'em."

Desdi reached the landing, where she could see Daventry's tall, elegant figure in riding dress. Facing him stood a small, rotund individual in a brown coat, buckskins, and boots that had seen considerable usage. He nodded his head of vivid red hair as he spoke, emphasizing his words. His rounded cheeks and merry eyes gave him an air of innocent childishness belied by the jut of a firm chin.

"This one, see—this one's all of a piece. Right within the radius, it is, though we ain't heard nothing of scouting the premises afore hand, we ain't. Still, that don't mean it ain't been done. Now, with your permission and all, we'll just set to work following those tracks and see if it leads us anywheres."

"Out toward the home farm, for a start," Desdi said, announcing her presence as she descended the last stairs.

The man regarded her through a pair of watery blue eyes. "And this will be the young lady as saw them?" he inquired.

"Very good." Desdi stepped forward, then turned for the earl to make the introduction. For a moment, she thought she glimpsed something in Daventry's eyes, a flash of pleasure, a spark of attraction, but it vanished at once—if it had ever been there at all. He continued to reject her.

His jaw tightened, lending him a grim, closed look. "Miss Lynton, this is Mr. Pimm, from Bow Street."

"A Runner?" That diverted Desdi's attention back to the little man.

"Yes, miss. Been down here nigh on two weeks now, and this news of yours is the best thing I've heard in that time. Now, with your lordship's permission, perhaps miss would be so kind as to show me where she saw these men and what they was about."

Desdi beamed at him, then caught sight of Daventry's stonelike countenance out of the corner of her eye. "I fear this takes precedence over our ride," she told him.

Her hopes of inducing a lighter mood in him faded. The sternness remained in his eyes, and tension drew the muscles tight in his jaw.

"I had not realized you intended to join me this morning," came his colorless response.

"Well, it seems to be of no matter now. Shall we go out at once?" She started for the door, very much aware of his following.

The barrier he had thrown up between them rose as tangible and forbidding as armor. It would not be easy to dismantle, but dismantle it, she would.

As they strode along the gravel path through the light covering of snow, she quickened her step to fall in at his side. "Something has put you out of temper," she informed him.

He looked down at her, exasperation patent on his angular features. "Has your aunt not explained to you that a young lady of breeding should not make personal comments?"

She considered a moment. "I don't believe so. Why?"

His mouth thinned. "You are an exasperating hoyden."

The words stung, but she forced her features into an expression of puzzlement. "I thought you said I was a young lady of breeding."

"I do not envy your aunt the handling of you." He turned to the Runner, asking him some question about the investigation.

Desdi allowed her steps to slow. Her aunt. Why did he speak of her aunt in such an assertive tone? Could it be—she broke off the thought, not wanting to face it, then forced herself to continue. Could he have made his decision? She adored her aunt Charlotte, knew no better or more capable woman existed. Her aunt could run his household to perfection. *But she is not the right lady for him.*

Desdi considered the matter, her aunt's patient good nature, her calm authority. She would make an excellent countess, but Daventry needed more than that. He might not realize it himself, but he'd seen too much war, too much destruction, too much death. He needed life and laughter, to be just a little frivolous. He needed *her.*

The intensity of that certainty startled her. He needed *her,* and if he offered for anyone else, even for dearest Aunt Charlotte, he would be making a dreadful mistake, as he'd come to realize all too soon.

He didn't look happy, not the way a man should look when he had chosen the lady he would love and cherish. She had to make him acknowledge it before it was too late. She eyed the back of his head as the earl stood with the Runner beneath the window of the west wing. She was not one to take defeat lying down. She would fight.

Fight. That sparked an idea so reprehensible it intrigued her.

The two men set forth in the direction of the home farm, the way she had seen those three figures disappear the evening before. She trailed after them, her thoughts drifting from the housebreakers to plans for Daventry's downfall. The men seemed to take no further notice of her, and for once that pleased her.

She really needed to draw Daventry away, separate him from the Runner. He would remain stiff and formal in the presence of the other man.

They trudged along the path leading beside the hedgerows that marked the farm boundaries. An exclamation of satisfaction escaped Mr. Pimm, and Desdi hurried to join them as they turned to follow another trail. There, by the side of the track, she could just make out the traces of booted feet that had crushed the snow and dried weeds into the mud.

She had followed this path before, she realized, on her first day here. It led over the footbridge, skirted the rectory, then led into the village, though she hadn't tramped all that way. Could the housebreakers be local men? Had they robbed first the houses at a greater distance from where they lived to avoid leaving a trail that would lead back to their doorsteps? If only this one would.

They crossed the stream, which glittered with the icicles that hung from every root and stem, and continued through the woods, frosted with snow.

At last they passed the line of trees and reached the small clearing. Across from them stood the hedge, its gate leading into the rectory yard. Here, the trail became unreadable. Any number of feet had passed this way, following the shortcut that led between the village and the small outlying farms beyond the ancient stone church.

"We should have come last night," Desdi declared in disgust as she eyed the trampled slush.

"I doubt me it would of done us any good, miss," declared Mr. Pimm, shaking his head. "This here path is so well used, there's a good chance as any clues might already have been destroyed." He eyed the short distance that separated them from the cobbled yard of the rectory's stable. "Think I'll just go and have a word with them as lives here," he announced. "Doubt they noticed anything amiss, but you never can tell. No, you never can tell."

Daventry drew out his pocket watch and frowned. "I'd best return to the house. The others will be up soon. If you learn anything, Mr. Pimm—"

But Desdi didn't stay to hear the rest of what he had to say. She slipped away, running lightly over the uneven path, ducking to avoid the sweep of wet limbs against her face. She didn't have much time, and her plan might well go dreadfully awry. But at least she would have tried.

"Miss Lynton?" His voice carried to her, sounding irritated. A pause, then he said, "Desdi?"

She made no answer. A large oak, bent and thick with age, loomed across the path, and she ducked behind it. Sufficient snow lay strewn across the ground for her purposes, and she scooped up an icy handful, patting it into a neat sphere, then waited, tossing it lightly from hand to hand to prevent her fingers from freezing.

The crunch of booted footsteps reached her first as he trod on icy patches and twigs alike. She held her breath, listening intently, gauging her timing. He neared her tree.

She sprang out, heaved her handful of snow, ducked back to scoop up another ball of icy crystals, then peeped around the trunk.

The earl stood stock-still in the middle of the path, an expression of such shock and outrage on his imperious countenance that she started to giggle. The look he directed at her should have laid her out, dead at his feet. She leaned against the tree, trying to control her mirth, as he glared at her.

"I—I am so sorry," she managed, struggling for breath. "I know I shouldn't laugh, but if you could only see your face. Do you not allow yourself to have any fun at all?"

"I do not," he said through clenched teeth, "consider being hit in the face with ice to be a source of amusement. Do you?"

"Indeed, yes. But you'll have to catch me to put it to the test." With that, she flung her next handful at him and darted down the path, laughing.

Less than five seconds later, something struck her full on the back. She spun to see him bent over, scraping the snow together for another missile. Stooping, she armed herself and let it fly without bothering to stand. He jumped sideways, and it swept harmlessly past to land in a holly shrub.

A gleam lit his eyes. Tossing the ball of snow from hand to hand, he advanced on her where she crouched to the side of the path. A gasp escaped her, half a giggle, half a surprised exclamation at the thoroughness at which he entered into her game. Without taking her gaze from his, she reached for more snow, throwing it at him without taking the time to pack it properly.

It disintegrated, only a few flakes splattering across his greatcoat. He stood before her now, drawing back his arm to heave his snowball at her at close range. She rolled, grasping up more handfuls, hurling them at him, reaching for more, even as he launched a gleeful, snowy revenge. She regained her footing, stumbled, and gasped once more as the snow struck her full in the neck.

Icy crystals seeped down the throat of her pelisse, but she had no time to waste on anything other than a renewed attack. She ducked behind the shelter of an elm to rearm herself, only to find him there before her. She took off running, laughing so hard she could barely keep her feet, with him in close pursuit, pelting her with snow at almost every step.

She reached a hickory, then fell against it, out of breath. Daventry stooped as he ran toward her, picked up one last handful, stumbled, and hurled his missile awry. Grinning, he fell against the tree at her side, staring down at her, his eyes dancing, his face flushed with the sheer exhilaration of their exercise.

The crystals that clung to her lashes melted, and she blinked away the moisture. With one finger, Daventry brushed the dampness away, then smoothed back her snow-wetted hair. "Hoyden," he accused, his voice a bare whisper.

His hand encircled the back of her neck, and for one glorious, suspended moment, she thought he would kiss her, longed for him to do so. She held her breath, gazing at him, her laughter stilling beneath the desire that surged through her, the wealth of emotion that left her weak, yet exultant. He gazed at her, an odd, yearning expression in his eyes.

Slowly—so slowly she thought he might never complete the motion—he leaned toward her until the warmth of his misting breath brushed her cheeks.

Abruptly he straightened. His hands caught her shoulders, and joy surged through her. He would drag her against him, hold her—

He turned her about and pushed her ahead, marching her forward, holding her at arm's length. "Back to the house with you," he said, though he could not disguise the shakiness of his voice. "What your aunt will have to say to you when she sees you like this, I shudder to think."

Eight

Daventry propelled Desdi forward, his hands clasping her shoulders, knowing he wanted to clasp her in a very different manner. All right, he wanted her.

He could no longer deny that fact, no longer convince himself it was naught but a passing fancy. He was no stranger to the company of ladies; he had, in fact, enjoyed a number of discreet liaisons over the long years of his campaigning. But not one of the objects of his gallantries, from that sloe-eyed Portuguese village girl to that Spanish contessa with skin like ivory, had aroused his passions as had this impish, ridiculous brat.

If he were still nothing more than Major Aubrey Kellands, he would turn her around, escort her to the rectory, and request that the elderly man post the banns at once.

But he was no longer a simple army officer. He was an earl, the head of his family, with tenants and servants and a position in the community that must, for the good of all, be maintained. He was not, he realized with a sense of consternation, for all his wealth and position, his own man.

Perhaps Desdi could be trained to the role his wife must play. Perhaps Xanthe would school the girl, bring out a serious, responsible side in her he had not yet glimpsed. Surely if she were not suitable, he would not care for her as he did, not love her so very much.

Love her. There, he'd admitted it, said the words, if only to himself. He loved her.

But a nobleman did not marry for love alone.

Try as he might, he could not envision her managing so great a household with any degree of order. Nor could he envision her successfully launching so inexperienced and uncertain a damsel as Bella into society. And as for Sophie, Desdi was far more likely to join in his younger half sister's scatter-brained larks than exercise any restraining influence over her.

These reflections sobered him, and he became aware of his drenched clothing, of the chill that seeped through every part of him. Desdi must feel equally uncomfortable. He fought back the impulse to cradle her in his arms, to warm her as best he could. Not now. Not yet. Possibly, the bleak thought struck him, not ever.

Yet how could he bear to let this laughing, loving child out of his life? He released her, and she fell into step at his side, skipping over puddles, dancing around shrubs that had grown up in the unkempt path. Her delight in discovering fun in everyday activities intrigued him anew, and he watched her, trying to see the world as the giant game she saw it.

An intriguing vision rose in his mind of approaching each new day as a fun-filled opportunity.

A retired major could do that. An earl could not.

Yet her musical laughter filled his mind, his heart, until it seemed nothing else mattered.

They let themselves into the house through the conservatory, where the muddied tracks of their drenched boots would not mar the pristine marble tiles of the entry hall. His stepmother had filled this vast chamber with plants, he remembered. Large, vigorous vines and shrubs had stood everywhere, the scent of their moist soil filling the air. Now only a few remained, and those looked brown and neglected, on the verge of dying. Desdi moved through the room swiftly, as if its atmosphere of decay and neglect repelled her.

As they crossed the corridor to the main hall, she dragged off her sodden pelisse, making an exaggerated grimace as she held it away from her. "Grisham will be dreadfully cross with me."

He smiled. "And so she should."

"I suppose your man takes this sort of thing in stride?"

He glanced down at his begrimed riding boots, muddied buckskins, and disreputable greatcoat. "Oh, he's had to deal with far worse during the course of our campaigning. Now, you'd best go to your room and do what you can to make yourself presentable, or no one will have left us anything for breakfast."

She started up the stairs with that light, dancing step that commanded his admiring gaze. As he set his hand on the banister to follow, a footstep sounded behind him, and he turned to see his majordomo approaching at speed.

The man cleared his throat, obviously uncomfortable with his errand. "If you please, my lord, I fear I must request a word with you." His lugubrious countenance revealed real consternation.

Daventry's heart sank anew. "What is it this time?"

Finley cast a meaningful glance at Desdi. "Perhaps it would be best, m'lord, if we were to step into another room."

"Oh, don't mind me," said Desdi brightly. But she made no move to join them, instead casting an apologetic glance at Daventry.

If his majordomo brought news of trouble in the house, as seemed likely, it might prove instructive to see how Desdi responded to it. Feeling somewhat guilty, as if he put a test before her, he returned his attention to Finley. "Let's have it. Is the house falling down about our ears?"

Finley's mouth pursed, but he otherwise betrayed no sign of disapproval. "Very good, m'lord. It seems Mrs. Seymour has been at the port and cannot be roused from her stupor. As this occurred before she had written the day's menus, Cook has gone off in strong hysterics, and several of the maids are threatening to quit. I thought you would wish to be informed as soon as you returned, m'lord."

"You did?" murmured Desdi. "I wonder why."

"The devil confound it!" exploded Daventry, glaring at his majordomo as if the messenger were responsible for the bad news. He drew a deep breath. He was better at handling several hundred soldiers than a handful of women. "Where is Lady Xanthe?" he demanded.

A certain morose pleasure showed in the major-domo's expression. "I fear she has driven out, m'lord, several of the young ladies having expressed a wish for an airing.

"The devil they did." Daventry stared at him blankly. "I don't suppose—" he began, then broke off as his gaze fell on Desdi.

She stood on the half landing, her hands clutching the banister, her lower lip clamped firmly between her teeth, her shoulders shaking with her repressed mirth. Outrage filled him that she could stand there laughing in the face of this complete disaster.

He had a house filled with guests who would remain for another four days. He had to see they were fed and cared for, the house cleaned, all duties—about which he realized he was abysmally ignorant—fulfilled.

Christmas was only two days away. How could the house be prepared, the feast made ready? His tenants would be calling, his guests would be in a festive mood, and there would be no food, no drink—no clean linens, for all he knew. And Desdi *laughed!*

"Shall we take turns cooking?" The girl's eyes brimmed with merriment. "We could each take charge of a meal. I daresay I could scramble eggs, if you didn't mind them charred just a little."

He stared at her. Could she do nothing better than make jokes? Lord, how could he have considered her suitable for so much as a single moment? He needed sober, useful support, not her hilarity and flippant suggestions.

She tilted her head to one side. "I could dust, but no one would wish to sleep in a bed I had made."

"Do you actually think you are being funny?" he demanded when he could command his voice. "Of all the childish, impossible, hen-witted, feather-headed, *useless* chits I have ever been saddled with, you are the worst. I should have thought a child of seven would have more sense and sensibility!"

He turned on his heel and strode off, shaken deeply by the pain of his disappointment, by the certain knowledge she was not the wife he needed.

Desdi watched him stalk across the hall and down the corridor that led toward his estate office. His words stung, but it was his reaction to the dire household news, rather than his hateful epithets, that tore at her. This wasn't the army, where every setback might mean life or death, where failure in duty could lead to the downfall of kingdoms. This was a country estate where the worst that could happen would be that a few guests might be discomforted for a day or two.

They'd survive. They'd undoubtedly sympathize, for domestic crises were not that uncommon, especially since Daventry had only just inherited a neglected household. If he could but see the humorous side of his situation, it could be solved so much more quickly and easily.

And solving was exactly what the situation needed at the moment. If matters weren't taken in hand at once, there would be no evening meal, not to mention the nuncheon to which she had begun to look forward since it seemed she had missed any chance of breakfast. She turned to the majordomo—Finley, wasn't that his name?—and found him regarding her with that bleak, mournful expression. "When is Lady Xanthe due back?"

A heavy sigh, redolent of long-suffering and impending disasters, escaped the man. "I really couldn't say, miss. Quite some time yet, I fear."

"But then you always fear the worst," Desdi pointed out. "Well, since no one else seems to be here, I suppose I shall have to intervene." She nodded to herself, coming to a decision, and fixed Finley with an amused but determined gaze. "You may escort me to the kitchens."

He blanched. "The kitchens, miss?"

She nodded encouragingly. "That's right. The kitchens."

"The—the kitchens," he repeated.

Desdi sighed. "Look, I think we've fairly well covered the destination. You just lead the way, and I'll follow."

"The kitchens," he said once more in failing accents.

"Never mind." Desdi patted him on the shoulder. "I think I can remember the way." And with that, she strode across the hall and down the corridor leading to the nether regions of the great, sprawling house.

Before she reached the green baize door leading to the servants' domain, Finley caught up to her. "Miss!" he protested. "You cannot—"

"Oh, his lordship won't mind," she declared with more airy assurance than she felt. He might mind her interference very much, indeed. After all, she hadn't the faintest notion what she would do when she had arrived at her destination. The thought of confronting a drunken housekeeper and a hysterical cook, demanding they return to their appointed duties upon the instant, made her giggle. She pushed through the door, turned left, and marched on with a sense of amused anticipation not untinged by a hint of uneasiness.

On her previous visit—the breakfast raid she had made in Daventry's company the morning before—she had gained the impression of a large apartment dominated by a massive hearth, copper pots hanging from the walls, herbs and onions suspended from the exposed rafters, and long oak tables laden with vegetables and roots. The air of efficiency which had hung over the room had now vanished. So, too, had the tyrannical and precise figure of the cook, who normally ruled these premises with an iron hand. The gaunt woman sat in a corner, her grizzled hair tucked untidily beneath a mobcap, her apron askew as she sniffled into the folds of a massive handkerchief. She didn't even look up as Desdi entered.

A petite scullery maid, her bright golden curls protruding from beneath her own mobcap, sat on the edge of one of the massive tables, swinging her legs saucily as she munched an apple. Before her stood a pot boy with a cinnamon bun in his hand. He glanced up at Desdi, and the pastry fell to the floor. The maid glanced over her shoulder, then sprang to her feet.

Arms akimbo, Desdi allowed her gaze to travel around the room, noting another maid, a young thing with wide, frightened brown eyes, kneeling just behind Cook. A third stood irresolute in a corner, her cap and apron in a heap on the floor before her, her gaze one of defiance. "I see," said Desdi slowly, and knew herself at a loss.

Aunt Charlotte would wade in, give a short rallying speech, and in minutes the kitchen would hum with its usual efficiency. Desdi hadn't the faintest idea what to say. She would probably make the situation worse. Looking about, she noted the slabs of bacon and a kettle of fish, and turned to the majordomo, who hovered at her shoulder. "What did everyone have for breakfast?"

"Cinnamon buns, miss. And tea. There was nothing else prepared."

Desdi nodded. "They'll be hungry when they return, then." She marched to the nearest table and picked up one of the potatoes that lay there. Dirt clung to it. Good heavens, what did one do with a potato? Cook it, of course—even she knew that. But how? And how many would the house party require for a nuncheon? But asking herself questions got her nowhere. She began heaping the roots into a large bowl, then carried it to the basin where pitchers of water stood ready.

"Miss!" protested Finley.

"Yes?" She glanced over her shoulder at him.

"You cannot!" he exclaimed.

She shrugged. "Someone has to." With that, she set to work scrubbing the potatoes. Not very efficiently, perhaps, but she hoped her vigor made up for any lack of finesse.

The maid who still held her apple core giggled, glanced at the outraged majordomo, and sobered at once. She scuttled forward to Desdi's side. "If you please, miss, I'll do that."

Desdi, trying not to let her relief show, stepped back, then turned her attention to the defiant maid who stood with her arms crossed before her, glaring at everyone in general. "Is there a ham that can be sliced?"

The girl sniffed. "That's not what we was planning for today."

"Well, it's probably what we're going to have, if there is one." She waited, but the maid said nothing more. She turned to the frightened girl who still knelt beside Cook. "You. Go see what can be assembled into a cold collation."

"Cold collation?" Cook looked up, her tear-blotched face darkening. "In December? What we need is a nice consomme, with a broiled chicken or two and maybe some thinly sliced beef in a wine sauce."

"Possibly," agreed Desdi, cheerfully. "But since I haven't the least idea how to prepare any of that, a cold collation it must be. You." She indicated the pot boy, who stared at her, mouth open, eyes bright, probably from the gossip he stored to relate at the taproom in the village inn that night. "Slice those carrots."

He stared at her as if she had run mad. "That's not my job, miss."

"It is now." She turned back to the maid, who remained beside the cook. "Where are the cooked meats kept? Never mind," she added, as the girl didn't move. "I'll find them myself." There had to be a larder somewhere; she couldn't imagine them simply shoving the perishable foodstuffs out the door into the snow.

Cook surged to her feet. "Here, don't you go waving my best carving knife at those carrots." She took it from the pot boy and replaced it in its holder. "Nancy, m'girl, you chop those carrots, and mind, I want them as thin as paper. Clara, when you've peeled those potatoes, you may put them on to boil. Quit playing with those knives, Thomas, and fetch me two bunches of parsley, one of thyme and one of marjoram. Jump to it, now." The servants jumped.

Cook surveyed her domain and nodded slowly. "Now then, miss." She turned to Desdi. "You go on back where you belong. And you may tell his lordship for me that some of us knows our duty. There'll be a meal set out as he can be proud of, in spite of this high and mighty new housekeeper of his."

Desdi, knowing herself evicted, beat a hasty retreat. Somehow she'd blundered into a way of dealing with the crisis and averted it.

Temporarily.

Xanthe followed the houseguests across the snow-strewn gravel as they returned from their outing. Actually, she floated a bare inch above the mired ground. After all, why should one dampen one's slippers if one could avoid it so easily?

Idly, feeling quite pleased with herself, she hummed a few notes, and the dirtied slush melted into tiny shimmering pools. Miniature golden fish, with puffy heads and long, trailing fins, leaped from one of these to another, leaving sparkling trails in their wake. Another few bars brought the rose bushes into full bloom, the sweetness of their scent permeating the chill air. Sometimes when she had worked a particularly clever or exotic bit of magic, she wished she could allow others to see her efforts. But sometimes not even the people she came to help appreciated her whimsies.

One particular example of that latter kind came to mind at once. Had Aubrey enjoyed the little surprise his household had held for him that morning? Little Desdi would.

She set a pair of bluebirds singing amid the lavender bushes that suddenly sprouted along the drive. A pair of peacocks appeared beside them, tails spread in their full glory. Definitely, the place needed a mistress who loved flowers and birds to rid it of its forlorn, abandoned austerity.

Titus appeared around the corner of the house, where he settled on his haunches. Just the tip of his tail twitched.

So Aubrey was in a rare taking, was he? That promised a lively interview. She shifted her gown into the semblance of a sail, hummed up a stiff breeze, and sped up the steps to the house. The majordomo held the door for her. The guests separated in the hall, some going to their chambers, some to the Blue Salon, some to the music room, some to the library.

Xanthe eyed Finley with amusement. "You look particularly gloomy this morning."

"As you say, madam." He hesitated, regarding her with those mournful eyes. "His lordship is wishful of speaking with you as soon as you are free."

"Is he?" Her amusement threatened to bubble over, and only with difficulty did she keep it in check.

"Yes, madam. In the estate office, if you please."

She hummed softly, regarded the man's resultant rabbit ears and whiskers with approval, and made her way along the corridor leading to the south wing.

She found Daventry seated at his desk, an untidy pile of papers before him, his hands pressed against the unruly curls at his temples as he leaned forward, staring into space. He looked up as she entered, but the sight of her seemed to afford him no pleasure. His bleak expression turned grim, and he glowered at her.

"You left on purpose," he accused her.

"I would hardly go out against my will," she countered.

"You are playing word games with me!" he snapped.

She beamed on him. "Games of any sort will do you a world of good, my dear boy." A few hummed notes escaped her, and a huge basket of flowers appeared on his desk. A vivid yellow canary landed on his head and proceeded to sing with all its heart.

He brushed it away. "Do you have any idea what chaos there has been?"

"A good deal, I should imagine. Did you not find it a delightful challenge?"

"Delightful! Lord, you're as bad as Desdi, and worse I cannot say! What the devil is there to find *delightful?*"

"Why, the chaos, of course." She hummed again, and half a dozen capuchin monkeys darted about the room, climbing the bookcases and swinging from the chandelier.

He closed his eyes. "I have a houseful of guests and a housekeeper who has drunk herself senseless and cannot be roused. My cook is in hysterics, the maids are threatening to quit, and you find it amusing."

She tilted her head to one side, considering. Another soft hum and the monkeys sported mobcaps and aprons, with little feather dusters in their hands.

He swore, displaying a breadth of vocabulary that commanded her admiration. Her eyebrows rose. "Well, at least you learned something of use with the army. How unique some of those words are. Portuguese, and some Spanish. Most original." She nodded in approval.

He stared at her in exasperation. "Can you never be serious?"

"And can you not learn?" she countered. "My dear Aubrey, can you not, just once, behave in a carefree manner?"

"When my party—*your* party, I should say—is threatened by the incompetence of my staff?" he demanded.

She gave an exaggerated sigh. "I ought to wash my hands of you. Yes, Aubrey." Her voice dripped patience. "Worry and ill-temper stifle creativity." A three-note hum produced a flourish of larks that swooped about the chamber, transformed into rose buds, then exploded in a shower of petals. "Be impulsive. You discover the most marvelous solutions that way." Another hum sent the papers swirling from his desk.

He started to grab at them, then sank back, watching through lowering brows as the sheets spun about in a lively reel. When they had settled once more—this time in neat piles—he said, "You suggest I take enjoyment in the discomfort of my guests?"

"Of course not, dear boy. I merely—"

"Then I have made my point." He rose. "I fear as long as I am entertaining, domestic order must be my top priority. This chaos cannot be allowed to continue." He nodded to her, then strode out the door, swinging it shut with a healthy bang.

Xanthe stared at the closed panel, frowning; then an impish smile tugged at the corners of her mouth.

As she hummed, the doorway faded, and the hall beyond became a sprawling meadow on which a dozen or more soldiers knelt, rifles raised and pointed at Xanthe. Daventry, in full uniform, astride his chestnut Clumsy, let out a shout, and his men charged forward, firing. . . .

The images faded. Xanthe shook her head, left a little rodent sprinting merrily in a wheel that Daventry alone would see next time he entered the room, and set off in search of Titus. They had a little magic to work. Since Daventry succumbed to the images people presented—and expected—she would encourage his guests to display their true natures. This would not be easy, but it would be a great deal of fun.

Nine

Desdi, in a becoming morning gown of pale blue merino and with a woolen shawl about her shoulders, descended the stairs shortly after noon. No angry shouting, no hysterical wails—in short, no sounds of domestic chaos—greeted her. Heartened that her foray into the kitchens had escaped censorious attention, she made her way to the breakfast parlor, where the footmen had arranged the gleaming chafing dishes over their tiny fires. A hot nuncheon it would be, it seemed.

Aunt Charlotte looked up from where she sat with Lady Eugenia, and the slight crease that furrowed her brow faded. "There you are, my love. I had quite thought you must have become lost while wandering in the woods."

"Something almost as much fun." Leaving her aunt to digest this tantalizing tidbit, she lifted the lid of a chafing dish and inhaled the delectable scent. How on earth had Cook managed to turn those ugly brown potatoes into anything so marvelous? The next dish revealed a chicken, sectioned and floating in a cream mushroom sauce. Desdi closed her eyes and inhaled. She would never take food for granted again, not after her brief brush with actually having to prepare it.

"Well?" demanded Aunt Charlotte as Desdi joined her at the table at last. "Are you going to explain?"

"What?" Desdi dragged her thoughts back from culinary matters. "Oh, this morning I met the most marvelous little man, a Mr. Pimm. Have you encountered him yet?"

"The Runner?" Lady Eugenia shuddered. "Mr. Eavesly pointed him out to me. Dreadful to be forced to have him about the estate."

"Oh? I thought it rather fun." Ignoring Lady Eugenia's shocked stare, Desdi regaled her aunt with a highly colored account of their trek through the trees and its unfortunate conclusion just short of the rectory. She didn't mention her snowball fight with Daventry; after all, it didn't really have anything to do with the topic.

As she finished, Lady Xanthe swept into the room, her expression more mischievous than ever. How, Desdi wondered, could anyone brighten a room with her mere presence? The woman seemed to make everyone happier just by walking in. Desdi wanted to laugh for the sheer joy of it.

"My love." Aunt Charlotte leaned across and smoothed one of Desdi's curls back into place. "When you go outside this afternoon—and I know you will, for nothing can make you stay indoors even in the most dreadful weather—be sure to wrap up warmly."

"Yes, dearest." Desdi rose, then stooped to drop

a kiss on the top of her aunt's head. "You need not fuss over me so, you know. I am quite grown."

"Yes." Aunt Charlotte sounded dubious.

"I don't know why you should want to go out," Lady Eugenia declared. "It is so very cold. Oh, I do wish we might have stayed in London over Christmas, for then we might have gone to visit the shops."

Desdi, who visited shops only at need, beat a hasty retreat. As she exited the parlor, she encountered Bertie Cumberland, Lord and Lady Lowestoft, and her father just about to enter. She greeted them, then escaped out of doors in search of Mr. Pimm and any news he might have.

She did not find him, but she did enjoy a long tramp through the woods. She followed their route of the morning, but when she reached the rectory she found no sign of anyone's being at home. She continued toward the village until she reached the yew hedge marking the border of The Larches, the cozy estate owned by Mr. Rackstraw, whom she had met at the ball.

Had the housebreakers prowled about his home as well last night? Mr. Pimm had undoubtedly asked, then inspected the grounds for any possible evidence or clues. Being a Runner sounded like such fun, though it undoubtedly had its uncomfortable side, too. Still, she would love an excuse to poke about asking questions, trying to solve some difficult and dangerous problem.

Laughing at her own absurdities, she turned about and started back. She saw no one on the return journey except the curate and two farmers who leaned against the top of a stone wall, gesturing into the distance. Desdi waved, and received an answering salute, but Mr. Beardsley didn't move to join her.

As she reached the edge of the home farm, she abruptly changed directions and veered toward the stable. She did not want to return indoors yet, not until the last vestiges of daylight had faded. Perhaps Daventry might be there, inspecting one or another of his horses, or another member of the party might be returning from a ride.

To her pleasure, she found Captain Frederick Grayson standing in the opening of a loose box. Inside stood a massive flea-bitten roan, a lanky animal with a Roman nose and his ears laid back flat. A groom leaned over at its side, holding up the right forefoot and rubbing his hand along the animal's tendon.

After a moment of careful pressing and probing during which the horse tossed its head and once snapped at him, the lad released the hoof. "Right you are, sir. Slight strain, no need to worry none. We'll just apply a poultice, and he'll be right as rain in a few days."

Captain Grayson stroked the animal's neck; it responded by butting his shoulder gently with its head. "I'll leave him in your hands, then." He turned and saw Desdi. "Rather cold to be out, is it not?"

She rolled her eyes. "You sound exactly like my Aunt Charlotte." To her surprise, a touch of color seeped upward from his collar.

"An inestimable woman," was all he said. He headed out into the yard.

Intrigued, Desdi fell into step beside him. Best not to pursue the subject of her aunt at once. "Did your horse fall?"

"My fault entirely," he said, with the true horseman's readiness to accept any and all blame when it came to his mount. "A rabbit hole or some such thing, covered by the snow."

"You're lucky you didn't take a tumble."

He shook his head. "Not on Rutherford. Never known a horse like him. He can carry me all day without a sign of weariness, not so much as a stumble. Lord, when I think of the country we traversed in Spain, with him never so much as throwing a shoe, and then I bring him back here and ride him into that damnable—I beg your pardon—that dashed rabbit hole. I'd never have forgiven myself if he'd come to grief."

She glanced at him, noting the seriousness of his expression. *A thoroughly nice gentleman,* she reflected. "My Aunt Charlotte is much that way, too," she said, speaking the thought out loud.

He stiffened, but she forged ahead. "She refuses to hunt, for she is forever in a quake that she might cause her horse to come a regular rasper at a gate. Which is nonsense, as I keep telling her, for she is a capital horsewoman. She never crams her fences, and she has never been ham-fisted. But she says one can never tell what may happen in the field, with so many people and hounds and horses."

"Very true." He kept his gaze ahead, not looking

at her. "Your father is very lucky to have her to keep house for him."

"Oh, she knows just how to order everything exactly as he—as any gentleman—could wish. But I know he feels guilty about her."

"Guilty?" Captain Grayson stopped and looked at her at last. "Whatever for?"

"For her not marrying, of course." They resumed walking. "She had enjoyed a couple of very successful Seasons in London, you must know, and he says she'd been on the verge of receiving not one but two very flattering offers when my mamma died. I was just in leading strings, and poor Pappa was quite devastated, so Aunt Charlotte simply turned her back on her own prospects, packed our bags, and brought us home to the country. And she's stayed, taking care of us both, ever since."

"She is an angel," Grayson breathed, with feeling.

Desdi peeped at him sideways. "The wish of Pappa's heart—and mine, as well—is that she might marry a good and honorable gentleman at last."

Grayson's steps quickened. "I believe—though I should not speak of it."

Desdi's glance darted to his profile. "Daventry, do you mean?"

He shook his head. "He has not spoken to me of his intentions." They neared the house, but he veered to a different path, taking them toward the rose garden. "Yet I can think of no more perfect wife for him."

Desdi's jaw tightened. "Suitable for a marriage of

convenience, perhaps. But I want so much more for Aunt Charlotte."

A hollow laugh escaped him. "My cousin is an excellent fellow, a matrimonial prize even without the earldom and all this." He waved his hand, indicating the estate.

"Worldly considerations have never influenced my aunt."

He shook his head. "They needn't. She seems to like him well enough."

"Liking is a far cry from loving," she pointed out.

A sad smile tugged at his lips as his gaze strayed to her face. "Loving is not necessary in a marriage where there is honest appreciation for one's partner's many excellent qualities."

This time it was Desdi who stopped. "Is that what you would want in a marriage?"

He waved his hand, a dismissive gesture. "I am not likely to marry."

He kept walking, but Desdi remained where she stood. "Why ever not? Because you believe the lady you love may be on the verge of accepting an offer from another?"

He halted, his back still to her, staring straight ahead. "It makes no matter why not."

"You love her, don't you? My aunt Charlotte?"

A moment passed before he turned to her, his features oddly tight. "My dear Miss Desdi—"

"Daventry doesn't love her. Would you be content to give her up to a marriage of convenience?"

"I would be content to see her happy."

"And who is to say she would not be happier with you?"

A sharp, painful laugh escaped him. "I have no chance to win her."

"But—"

He held up his hand, silencing her. "A one-armed man with no rank or fortune to recommend him?"

"You have a home, do you not?"

"Nothing to compare with Kellands Court."

"Do you think that would matter to her?"

"If she were to love me—" He shook his head. "But I have no reason to believe she could."

"You could ask her."

"A fine cake I would make of myself. No, her brother is very much in favor of a match with Daventry. And who can blame him?"

"Me," muttered Desdi, but under her breath. She considered a moment. She had seen Grayson and her aunt together, walking about the garden, talking in the evening. A bond existed between them, but in truth she didn't know whether her Aunt Charlotte regarded him in the light of a suitor or as the cousin of the gentleman she hoped to marry. Suddenly, it became imperative she find out.

She went to the music room in search of her aunt, and found instead Daventry, who stood on the far side of the room staring out the window. She hesitated in the doorway, gazing at him, aware of his height, the breadth of his shoulders, the understated elegance of his appearance. Aware of *him*.

Several long seconds passed before the discordant notes of a harpsichord penetrated her absorption. An elderly man, bearing all the appearance of a neat clerk, sat at the ancient instrument in the corner, his delicate fingers now pressing the individual keys that in turn caused each string to be plucked. He paused after each note while he seemed to listen and consider. At last he nodded, opened the instrument, and reached inside.

Desdi strolled forward. "Tuning?"

The earl glanced at her. "My stepmother adored that instrument. I doubt it's been touched since her death." He led her from the room, leaving the little man to his labors. "Were you looking for me?"

"My aunt, actually." Yet now she was with him, she only wanted to remain, to experience that odd thrill that raced through her at the sound of his deep voice, to try to bring a smile to his harassed eyes.

The frown in them deepened. "I do not believe I have seen her this afternoon."

"It doesn't really matter." She tilted her head to one side. "You will do. We need to rehearse."

A sudden, wry smile tugged at the corners of his mouth. "We need to avoid performing altogether."

She shook her head. "And you need not think we will change our scene so you may play a corpse."

That stopped him. "What a perfectly clever idea. I wish I had thought of it at once."

"Too late now. We are committed to *Romeo and Juliet,* and *not* the death scene. And I think you have gotten off very lightly, considering what the others are trying to do."

Aunt Charlotte, she remembered suddenly, had drawn Captain Grayson for her partner. If only they played a love scene! For that matter, if only she and Daventry had not decided to play their love scene for laughter. Ah, for lost opportunities.

She took the earl by the arm and drew him into the next room, only to encounter Lady Eugenia and Sir Joshua, hard at work on their own skit. Desdi apologized, and withdrew with her captive to the next chamber.

"At least I may stop worrying about the quality of my performance," Daventry said.

Desdi caught his glance and burst out laughing. "Let us be as bad as we possibly can!" she suggested. "It will go with our comic approach, and no one can pity us for our lack of acting ability." With that, to her utter amazement, he agreed. He started their scene with something actually approaching enjoyment, and Desdi lost herself in the delight of simply being with him.

A gong sounding somewhere deep within the house startled her some time later. With sincere regret, she parted from Daventry to head for her chamber and dress for dinner. She still hadn't spoken to Aunt Charlotte, she remembered with a touch of guilt as she changed into her gown of pomona green muslin. Gathering her woolen shawl about her shoulders, she started for the door.

A glance at the mantel clock assured her she had delayed too long in the earl's company, and her aunt must already have gone downstairs. She found her in the Blue Salon, seated on a sofa between Lady Eugenia and Harriet Eavesly.

Charlotte waved to Desdi but showed no inclination to leave her companions. Not that they could have a quiet word in here, Desdi reflected, and almost begrudged her late afternoon's stolen rehearsal with Daventry. But time with him she could never regret. She would simply have to wait until after dinner, if not until after they had all retired to their beds.

Yet waiting became more difficult. She could not help but be aware of Captain Grayson, of the way his gaze strayed to Aunt Charlotte, or the light that flickered in his eyes whenever she smiled. She would make the perfect wife for him, if she could return his regard.

Of course, Charlotte would make the perfect wife for any gentleman, Desdi reflected, watching her aunt's easy grace and elegant demeanor. But Captain Grayson loved her, and she would swear Daventry, whatever his intentions might be, did not.

Desdi barely tasted her meal, so closely did she watch Charlotte. Yet that lady's well-bred manners defied Desdi's attempts to determine her preferences. Not by so much as a single glance did she betray any telltale interest in any of the gentlemen at the table. When the meal at last drew to a close and the ladies withdrew, Desdi managed to position herself at her aunt's side.

Charlotte looked down at her with a thoughtful frown. "Do you have the headache?"

Desdi blinked. "Why, no."

"Then perhaps you are sickening for something?"

A short laugh escaped Desdi. "Whatever do you mean, dearest aunt? Do I look unwell?"

Charlotte draped an arm about her shoulders. "You have been staring at me ever since you came down to dinner. If you are not unwell, then what is troubling you?"

"Nothing. I only—" She broke off, for her ready tongue could find no excuse but the truth.

"Something momentous is on your mind," Charlotte declared. "You are not growing bored, are you?"

"Far from it," Desdi assured her, startled.

Charlotte nodded. "Then what is it you wish to speak to me about?"

"Nothing in particular," Desdi tried, but it sounded false to her ears.

Her aunt regarded her with that gentle amusement that told her, quite clearly, she fooled no one.

"It has been a very pleasant time, has it not?" she tried.

"Very," Charlotte agreed promptly.

"The company is most agreeable," pursued Desdi.

"Most," Charlotte agreed again. She offered no leads, no help at all.

Desdi fell silent. She would bide her time. The opportunity would come. She had only to pounce on it when it did.

A good portion of the evening passed before her long-sought opening arrived, and then she almost missed it. Captain Grayson, rising from the card table where he had played at piquet with Sir Joshua, stooped to pick up a ball of yarn that had rolled from Mrs. Marcome's lap. Desdi saw him return it to her, shifted her attention back to the card house she watched Daventry construct with Sophie and Bella, then abruptly realized her chance had presented itself.

"He is so very kind," she whispered to her aunt, beside whom she had stationed herself all evening in the hope of just such an opening.

"Who is?" Charlotte whispered back.

"Why, Captain Grayson, of course." Desdi cast a sideways glance at her aunt. "He is forever doing little things to help people."

"Yes, indeed." A troubled expression flickered across Charlotte's face.

"He would make the most delightful husband, do you not think?" Desdi pursued. Charlotte's brow creased, and Desdi feared she had gone too far. "I mean—" she began, but Charlotte's gentle, concerned smile stopped her.

"Are you in danger of developing a *tendre* in that quarter, my dear? It is no surprise, to be sure. But a gentleman who is all consideration, all goodness, whose manner and address must universally please, might have his little attentions misunderstood. Then woe to the lady who has given her heart too quickly."

Desdi flushed. "It—it is no such thing, I assure you. But only fancy his difficulty if the lady he fancied merely thought him being pleasant and nothing more."

Charlotte smiled that sad smile again. "A gentleman must make his attentions clear if he wishes to fix a lady's interest."

Desdi regarded her intently. "What would you recommend?"

"I?" Charlotte laughed. "I am no gentleman."

"But what would you suggest a gentleman as generally considerate as Captain Grayson do if he wished to fix his interest with a lady—with you, for example?"

She shook her head. "You are quite absurd, my love. Now, I must have a word with Mrs. Marcome." She rose. "And if he does try to fix his interest with you, I make no doubt your pappa will approve."

Desdi slumped back against the cushions, watching her aunt's graceful figure move across the drawing room. She hadn't gained anything from that at all, except to put the idea into Charlotte's head that Desdi herself might care for Captain Frederick Grayson. What a muddle she had made of it all.

And the worst of it was she couldn't even tell if her aunt minded. Perhaps the captain was right, and Charlotte had no interest in him beyond the merest friendliness. In that case, she might well have made up her mind to marry Daventry if the earl should ask her. Depressed, Desdi retired early to her chamber.

She found it difficult to sleep, though. She lay in her bed, her fingers plucking disconsolately at the coverlet, replaying in her mind every word her aunt had spoken, every expression that had flitted across her face. No, she simply couldn't tell.

Tomorrow, she reflected with growing depression, would be Christmas Eve, and they would give their skits, and her own special partnering with Daventry would be over. Then would come Christmas, when he would be busy with his tenants and the neighboring landowners coming to call. Then would come Boxing Day and the party would break up, and perhaps he would offer for Aunt Charlotte, and she would have to go on seeing him as her uncle, when she wanted so very much more from him. . . .

Moisture brimmed in her eyes, but she blinked it back. More fool she, to give way to tears. She hadn't lost yet. And as much as she loved Aunt Charlotte, she loved Daventry more.

She must have drifted off to sleep at last, for the barking of dogs from outside, followed by shouts and the muffled sound of a pistol going off, sent her sitting bolt upright in her bed. The housebreakers. They must have come back. The commotion continued, at a distance but unmistakable, and she shoved her feet into slippers and grabbed her dressing gown. Dragging it on, she ran down the hall, determined not to miss out on the miscreants' capture.

Ten

The other doors on the corridor remained closed. Hadn't they heard? Desdi wondered. But probably everyone else slumbered deeply, not kept on the verge of wakefulness by uncertainties and longings.

Still, someone must be awake besides herself, for the housebreakers—if it were indeed they—would not fire pistols at one another. Daventry must have set someone to watch for them, to patrol the grounds against the possibility the miscreants should return.

She had started down the stairs, her shawl draped over one shoulder, when the sound of footsteps running behind her brought her to a halt. Daventry, his hair tousled, his greatcoat hanging about him as he struggled into it, appeared from a side corridor, only to come to an abrupt halt at sight of her. "Go back to your bed," he ordered, and pushed past.

Desdi didn't waste time arguing; she just ran after him. "Do you know what happened?"

"I set the grooms to keep watch. Go back to your bed."

A pounding came on the front door. Daventry reached it first, slid back the bolt, and dragged it open. An odd, bulky shape stumbled in, grotesque in the wavering shadows. Desdi grasped a candelabrum, thrust one taper into the flame of a softly glowing oil lamp, then lit the other branches. As the light increased, she recognized the figure as one of the grooms.

"They come back, m'lord," the little man gasped. "Five of 'em, there was. 'Ad the window pried open, they did, and one of 'em 'ad 'is leg over the sill when we come up on 'em. Me and Sammy, we tried to hold 'em up, but they tipped us the double and made off."

"Were either of you hurt?" Daventry demanded.

The man wrinkled his cold-reddened nose. "No. 'Twas Sammy as let off his popper. Give 'im a right box to the ears, I did, too, for missing 'em."

"Where's Sammy now?" Daventry asked.

"Still at 'is post." He snorted. "Just you sees what I does if 'e tries to 'are off."

Finley, wrapped in a brocade dressing gown of a resplendent purple, hurried down the corridor. "I heard a knock—" He slowed as he beheld the groom.

Daventry glanced at Finley. "Send Robert or William to the stables to rouse one of the other grooms. I want him to ride to the inn and bring Mr. Pimm back.

"Come on, Hewlett." He turned to the groom again. "Let's see what we can discover."

A blast of icy wind swirled into the hall as they exited. Desdi shivered. Yet if she returned upstairs for her cloak, she would probably miss everything.

Wrapping her shawl about her head and shoulders, she set off in the men's wake.

Daventry glanced back as she caught the door he'd started to close, and his brow snapped down. "Go upstairs."

"There's no danger. The housebreakers are gone."

"You'll freeze," he shot back. "Finley, see to it Miss Lynton does not follow us." With that, he departed.

She glared at the door as it slammed behind him, and turned her mulish expression on the poor majordomo.

The distressed man cleared his throat. "If you please, miss?"

"Oh, go run your errand," she snapped, and turned toward the stairs.

The man hesitated, but by the time she had reached the first landing, she could hear his retreating footsteps as he went to rouse the other male servants.

She returned to the hall and considered. She faced south now. That meant she had only to follow that corridor to her right, past the ballroom, and she'd come to the section that had been closed by the earl's father.

She set down the candelabrum, selected a single candle, and placed it in one of the holders that sat on the table. Protecting its flame with one hand, she ran lightly along the carpeted hall until she reached a closed door. It opened with a blast of chilled, stale air and a protesting squeak, and she darted a nervous look over her shoulder to see if anyone heard. But Daventry had never forbidden her this approach.

Huddling into her shawl, she pressed on, opening first one door and then the next, until she found a darkened room in which the scent of fresh pine dispelled the aura of disuse. She made her way about the outer edge, avoiding the furniture that had been piled into the center of the room and shrouded beneath Holland covers. Shadows fled against the walls as she passed, lurking, threatening like ghostly figures or—

She cast an uneasy glance over her shoulder. None of the housebreakers had actually entered the room, had they? Could one be hiding here, awaiting his chance to escape? She shivered.

"Don't you take another step!" a quavering voice cried.

Desdi froze, her heart pounding so loudly that for a moment she could hear nothing else.

Then the voice came again from outside. "Mr. Hewlett! Mr. Finley! I caught one of 'em. 'E's moving about in that room, 'ere. I can see 'is light!"

Desdi's knees buckled, and she leaned against the sheet-covered back of a chair, all that held her upright. Not one of the villains.

But very possibly worse, she realized the next moment. This must be the shooting-happy Sammy. She could only hope he possessed just the one pistol, the one he had already discharged. Of course, he might have had time to reload it.

"You!" came the quavering voice again. "I got

me barker pointed right at you. Don't you move none."

She couldn't make out his figure; her light threw all beyond its range into impenetrable darkness. She opened her mouth to tell him who she was, but footsteps approaching at a run caused him to back a few paces from the window.

"Sammy?" she tried, but her voice came out a croak that could not have carried to him.

"You got one of 'em?" came Hewlett's excited shout. "Don't you go shooting 'im, now. Not till we 'as our chance to shake all the information out of 'im."

"Thank you, Hewlett," came Daventry's amused drawl. "I believe we shall have him out here."

"Why not come in here?" Desdi managed to call.

Complete silence greeted her sally. She ventured a step, and no orders came from Sammy for her to remain still. Emboldened, she crossed to the window and held up her candle. "It is not much warmer in here, but at least there is less wind."

Daventry swore softly.

"A *female?*" Hewlett stared at her, indignant. "Now if that don't beat the Dutch."

"A lady," the earl corrected him gently. "One of our guests, to be precise. Miss Lynton, may I assume my zealous groom has been holding you at pistol point?"

"A most unique experience, I assure you." The brightness of her response pleased her; it would have mortified her to have given in to the hysterics that for one brief moment had threatened.

"And I believe we can assume you are alone?" the earl continued.

"Well, I only arrived a few moments ago, but I don't think there is anyone else here. You are welcome to come in and search."

Daventry picked his way through the shrubs that lined the wall; she could hear the snapping of twigs as he positioned himself at the window. Even with his height, his shoulders barely showed.

"It might be an excellent notion," he said, then chuckled as she cast an involuntary glance over her shoulder. "At last, I see you discomposed. My dear Miss Lynton, I did not believe it could be done."

"Unhandsome," she declared. "But if you are to come in, I would recommend doing so through the house. It is much easier."

"But it would take more time." His hands rested on the sill, and abruptly he jumped, straightening his arms until he swung himself to sit on the ledge. In another moment he had lowered himself inside.

From beneath the window came the sounds of an argument as Hewlett tried to convince Sammy to boost him after his master, and Sammy's averring that he was trying. "Try harder," hissed Hewlett.

Daventry leaned out, holding down a peremptory hand. After a moment the groom took it, and Daventry dragged the little man into the room.

"It might be more to the point to look about outside for any traces," Desdi said. "If someone had gotten in here, he might well have moved on to another part of the house by now."

Daventry scowled at her. "We shall have to rouse

everyone, I suppose. What a fine way to treat my guests."

Desdi shook her head. "They would far rather be roused by a member of your staff than by some desperate villain." She shivered, hugging her shawl close about her. Her teeth began to chatter.

Daventry muttered an oath and dragged off his greatcoat. "Here, you vexatious brat." He arranged it about her shoulders.

"Now you'll freeze." She hadn't cared for his manner of addressing her; it fell somewhat short of the loverlike endearments she longed to hear from him. Yet his kindness in giving her his greatcoat, still warm from his body, helped ease the sting.

"If you went back to your bed, where you belong, it would solve both our problems."

"What? And possibly encounter some thief who has taken refuge there? I shall be much safer helping."

He regarded her with a mixture of exasperation and amusement. "You never give up, do you?"

"Why on earth should I?"

He took her with him to find the majordomo and instigate a search of the premises. Desdi stood just behind him in the hall, listening with only half an ear to the orders he issued. She didn't really believe anyone had gotten inside. If someone had, it would have been an easy matter to escape once Hewlett had gone for help and only Sammy had stood guard. Therefore, if anyone wanted to discover anything, they ought to search outside, while the tracks remained fresh.

She felt certain she knew which path they would follow. The only question in her mind was which direction they would take when the path separated at the rectory. She could think of only one way to find out.

Everyone would be too busy for a while to accompany her. She looked down at Daventry's greatcoat that she still wore, then at her slippered feet. They were sturdy slippers. They'd do. She wasn't about to let her opportunity slip. Those thieves had taken her mother's jewelry case, and she wanted it back. If it were already gone beyond her reach, well, she would have a hand in the downfall of the men who had taken it.

She slipped out the door and made her way to the stables. There'd be a lantern there, one with a hood so she could direct the light where she wanted it and not make a beacon of herself. As she neared, she could hear the rustling sounds of the disturbed horses as they shifted on their straw. Poor things, they probably weren't accustomed to such nighttime annoyances.

She found several lanterns hanging in a row in ready reach. She chose the nearest, found it to be full of oil, and adjusted the shutter so only the thinnest beam guided her feet. Pleased with herself, she set forth at a brisk pace to do what she felt the others ought to be doing.

She didn't slow until the babbling of the stream reached her, long before it came into sight. *Such a peaceful sound,* she reflected. She looked up into the night sky, but no stars glittered in the velvet, deep purple darkness. Even as she watched, it faded to the dark blue that presaged dawn.

Dawn. She'd never stopped to look at a clock. It would be morning soon, which meant it would be easier to find traces in the snow. And she would see them before the sun had a chance to rise and melt them with warming rays. Really, she couldn't have timed this better. For now, though, she must still use the lantern, for beneath the trees it remained as murky as midnight.

With a sense of relief, she emerged at last into the clearing by the rectory wall. She set the lantern down and moved to the side of the path, careful not to disturb the remaining snow and mud.

Several people had trodden this route since the sun last warmed it. She guessed the trail would lead away from the village, but to her surprise, only older markings marred the slushy patches in that direction. Frowning, she started forth toward the village, only to come to an abrupt halt before she had gone more than a dozen paces. No tracks—at least, none that seemed recent.

She crept farther, searching from side to side, in case the men had walked through the twigs and bracken. They hadn't. She turned about slowly, studying the surrounding area. That seemed to leave the gate into the rectory's stable yard. Had those brazen villains dared to cross the sanctuary grounds in order to elude any possible pursuers? She moved to the gate, unlatched it, and swung it wide.

Within, muddied footprints marred the normal tidiness of the cobbled yard. They led, in fact, to the low stone stable. Her first thought, that Mr. Beardsley had made them when he returned from visiting one of the distant farms, wavered. There were too many of them, too much mud. Nor had a horse's hooves caused them; she could make out the definite imprint of boots.

She peered through the semidarkness, following the tracks with her gaze. She hadn't been mistaken. They led to the low-pitched structure where Mr. Beardsley's cob and the rector's carriage horse were stabled.

Desdi started forward, uncertain, cautious. This couldn't be the right trail; she must have gotten it confused. No one could use the rectory grounds for any illicit purpose. Even if the rector were too vague to notice what occurred in his own yard, others busied themselves about the church and the rectory— Mr. Beardsley, their housekeeper, and any number of their parishioners.

But what if several of the parishioners had made the stable their special duty? What if they had converted it to their own illicit purpose, with the clerics none the wiser? After all, how often would either of those two men enter the stables, especially if someone from the village, a member of their flock, someone they trusted, offered to perform such services for them?

And if they stored their stolen goods here? She eyed the low stone building. At one end two narrow windows stood barely above ground level. The storage side, with a basement beneath. If the villains used that basement, secreting their stash securely out of the way, a chance visit on the part of Mr. Beardsley would prove no danger to them. Suddenly, it all seemed too possible.

She stopped, knowing that to go forward would be foolhardy. She should go back, tell Daventry of her suspicions, make him listen to her, convince him to help her investigate. If she were right, if they found any evidence, they could alert Mr. Pimm and lay a trap to discover who was involved.

Now, to get out of here before anyone saw her and asked why she prowled about at so early an hour. She turned to retrace her steps, only to find herself facing a greatcoated figure leaning against the open gate, his hat pulled low over his face.

Desdi froze, her heart pounding, then forced a wavering smile to her lips. "You startled me." She should probably walk toward him in a casual manner, but she couldn't bring herself to move any closer.

He studied her, his eyes cold slits of light in the growing dawn. "Now, what brings a nice young lady like you out so early? And all dressed up in your night things, too, by the look of it."

She stared at him while her mind raced, fastening at last on the only plausible response. "I have urgent need of the rector. What brings *you* out?"

He ignored her counterattack. "Rectory's that way." He jerked his head toward the ivy-covered house beyond a hedge-lined brick wall. "Can't see what you'd want in the stable."

"I was just finding my way," she said with what

hauteur she could muster. "I have only been in the area a few days."

He straightened. "Why didn't someone send a servant?"

"I—I didn't think. And now I am wasting precious time." She turned from him, only to be brought up short by the sight of another man just emerging from the stable door, a gleaming silver candelabrum in one hand. He stopped at sight of her. "What the devil?"

"Put that thing back!" the first man snapped. He moved from the gate, closer to Desdi, but still in the direct line of any hope of escape.

The second man remained where he was. "What's she doing 'ere, 'Arry?" he demanded.

"Come for the rector," supplied Harry. "At least, that's what she says."

Desdi swallowed. "And I really must go to him now."

"No, you don't." Somehow, Harry had reached her, and his hand closed over her elbow. His fingers bit into her arm, even through the heavy fabric of Daventry's greatcoat.

She straightened, feigning an outrage she hoped disguised her fear. With her voice dripping ice, she said, "Let go of me."

"All in good time, missy." He regarded her with a frown.

"Who is she?" The second man, the candelabrum hanging loosely in his hand, joined them.

"One o' the guests at the big 'ouse, I'd reckon." The two exchanged glances.

"Well, I suppose we knows what dragged 'er out o' 'er beauty sleep." The second ran a hand over his stubbly chin.

"How could you possibly know?" Desdi demanded. "If you must have it, though I cannot see where it is any of your concern, my aunt took ill."

"Seems as if a doctor would of been more to the point," said Harry.

"Aye." The second nodded. "Old rector, 'e wouldn't be of no 'elp."

"None at all," agreed his companion.

" 'Less she got 'erself 'it by that pistol as went off and thought as 'ow she was gonna die," the second man suggested.

"We got ourselves a visitor?" demanded a new voice.

Desdi turned, and to her dismay saw a third man emerge from the stable, garbed in rough clothes similar to the other two. He carried a small chased silver urn in his hand.

"Where you goin' with that, Bert?" Harry demanded. "Thought as 'ow we wasn't goin' to sell none of that lot as of yet."

"Just admirin' it, like," said the new arrival. "What you plannin' on doin' with 'er?"

That question had been exercising Desdi's mind for some time. "You might let me complete my errand to the rector," she said, though she knew it for a forlorn hope.

"Can't let 'er go," mused the second man. "She'd 'ave that Runner down on us 'fore the cat could lick its ear."

Desdi considered keeping up her pretended lack of comprehension, but a glance at the harsh faces surrounding her warned her it would do no good. She kept silent, hoping against hope for a stroke of luck.

"Could shoot 'er," suggested Bert, with the pride of one suggesting a brilliant idea.

"What, an' bring the ol' rector down from the 'ouse?" demanded the second. "Squeeze 'er neck— that's the ticket."

Harry ran his gaze over her. "Might be worth somethin' if we kept 'er safe and quiet."

"What do you mean?" Bert peered at him, frowning.

"Might be someone willing to pay a bit to get 'er back all safe and sound," he explained.

The second man's eyes gleamed. "Worth a tidy bit, wouldn't you say?"

"Aye." The third man dragged the syllable out, considering. "She can't cause us no 'arm after tomorrow, anyways, if we get this all cleared out tonight." He looked at his two comrades. "And we'd 'ave ourselves a little somethin' to set us up 'til we can unload this lot."

All three regarded her.

"Little extra money never 'urt no one," said Bert. He reached toward her, and Desdi flinched away. His fingers grasped the fine gold chain that suspended her mother's locket about her neck, and with a jerk he tore it free. "Just to let your family know as 'ow we really got you." He held up the gleaming oval, twisting it so the rising sun sent sparkles glinting from it.

"Where we gonna put 'er?" asked the second.

Harry considered. "Cellar," he decided after a moment. "Gag 'er so she can't make no fuss."

From close by came the squeak of an opening door. Desdi stiffened, but the man who held her clamped a greasy hand over her mouth and dragged her back toward the shrubbery that lined the rectory wall. Someone came, someone these horrible men might not hesitate to hurt. Poor old Mr. Doncaster—

With all her might, she brought her foot down on the boot of the man who held her. A sharp exclamation escaped him; then he grabbed her savagely, sweeping her off her feet, never moving his hand from her mouth. She tried to bite him.

"Want me to throttle you?" his voice hissed in her ear.

She subsided, hoping she had done enough to warn whoever came out that someone lurked just around the corner.

Footsteps approached, and the second man drew a pistol from his voluminous coat pocket. Silent screams of warning filled Desdi, painful to hold back. Then Mr. Beardsley, a gray greatcoat pulled over his clerical black, strode around the corner, only to stop at sight of them. His gaze took in the group.

Tears of dismay stung Desdi's eyes. She hadn't saved him. He'd be captured—or killed, as they could hope for no ransom for him. If only she'd struggled harder.

"What the devil do you mean by this?" the curate demanded, outraged. "Can't you three do anything without turning it into chaos? Lord, when I think of the trouble I've gone to. What is she doing here?"

He was one of them. The truth struck Desdi, leaving her weak. One of them? No, more than that. He must be their leader.

"Found 'er prowlin' about, we did." The man set her back on her feet, but kept one hand on her mouth and his other arm tight about her waist.

"So you had to immediately make it clear she'd stumbled onto something? Have you no sense at all? I'm not ready to leave here yet."

The third man stared at him with the expression of one trying to understand. "You gave orders as we was to clear out the cellar."

Mr. Beardsley drew in a long breath. "Lord, give me patience," he muttered. "I never said we were leaving, though it looks like now we'll have to. My dear Miss Lynton, I fear you are proving a grave inconvenience and causing me a great deal of trouble."

Desdi tried to open her mouth, but her captor's hand held it firmly shut.

Mr. Beardsley sighed. "A great deal of trouble," he repeated. He glared at the three men. "And just what," he asked with heavy sarcasm, "did you plan to do with her?"

"The cellar." The men looked relieved to be back on firm ground. "Tie 'er up and stuff a rag in 'er mouth, and she'll keep all right an' tight 'til someone forks over the ready so's we'll set 'er free."

Mr. Beardsley's eyes widened. "Ransom. Well, well. Perhaps I've misjudged you." His eyes clouded with thought. "Yes, that will sweeten the pot, I should think. It will even smooth our way into another county. Perhaps we will leave after all."

He blinked and looked at them once more. "To the cellar with her, then, and make sure you secure her properly. We don't want her getting out and spoiling everything." He touched her cheek with one finger. "It would be a shame to have to kill you, my dear, but we will if you cause us any trouble. A ransom would be nice, but not worth it if you create a risk. Enjoy your stay as our guest." He led the way toward the barn.

Desdi's captor swung her back into his arms and carried her the short distance, ducking low to ease them through the doorway into the chill, dank sideroom smelling of leather and mildew where the tack was stored. One of the others produced several lengths of fine, stout rope, and within minutes they had bound her wrists behind her. Mr. Beardsley raised a trapdoor in the corner, and dank air rushed up to greet her. She shivered.

"It won't be for long," Mr. Beardsley assured her, amused. "No more than a day or two, I should think. Your father will want you back, won't he?"

She glared at him, but he merely pushed her forward. She stumbled, caught her balance, then submitted to being led down the stairs.

Light penetrated from the narrow windows, illuminating dust motes. The air smelled heavy with dirt and damp, and the sticky tendrils of torn spiderwebs brushed her cheek. An assortment of small trunks and crates lined the walls. The objects they had stolen, she presumed, neatly packaged for safe transportation. One portmanteau stood open, and something metallic gleamed within.

She looked about, then managed to curl her lip in what she hoped was a contemptuous sneer and not an expression of panic. "I cannot say I think much of your accommodations."

"I am sorry, my dear." Mr. Beardsley smiled. "You should have sent ahead to warn us of your intentions of paying us a visit. Never mind. We shall just have to make do."

"I could make do with breakfast," she suggested.

He stared at her. "Well, we shall have to see what—if anything—can be done. But for now, my dear, I must bid you farewell. Gag her," he said over his shoulder, and remounted the steps.

Desdi regarded the three remaining men with no little trepidation. The first rammed a stinking, foul-tasting rag into her mouth, then secured it with another, which he knotted behind her head, entangling her hair in a very painful manner. Bert dropped to one knee before her, grabbed her ankles in his rough hands, then secured them with another length of rope.

"No sense tryin' to get away," Harry warned her. "Ain't no use." With that, her captors departed.

When the last one stepped through the trapdoor, they lowered it behind them, and she could hear the sound of a bolt being drawn into place. Even if she managed to maneuver her way up the stairs, she would not be able to break through to the saddle room. She hopped to the side of the cellar, seated herself on a closed trunk, and looked about her dank, freezing prison. She felt dangerously close to tears.

Eleven

Daventry paced the length of the upper corridor, glancing from doorway to doorway as he went. He and the servants had checked every room, disturbed his no-longer-slumbering houseguests, and had found no intruder. The presence of one, of course, had never been more than a remote possibility, but one he had to check. He could only regret disturbing the entire household for what had proved to be a false alarm. His guests would probably think twice before accepting another invitation from him.

Which, he supposed, had a certain advantage to it, for he found entertaining to be a considerable interruption to all he needed to accomplish.

One of the doors behind him swung wide, and he turned to see Colonel Marcome, garbed in a mulberry velvet dressing gown, thrust out his head. "Daventry!" the man shouted. "Been ringing for my man for the devil of a long time, but no one comes." He regarded his host with an accusing glare, as if Daventry could have arranged such an occurrence for the sole purpose of annoying him.

"They might not yet be back from their search.

Try again in a few minutes," Daventry suggested, then set forth to make certain this time the colonel's summons would not go unanswered.

There must be any number of other domestic amenities disrupted by the predawn furor, he reflected with a touch of unease. A housekeeper, or a capable mistress of the establishment, would have had things running smoothly again within minutes. He lacked both. Which, he supposed, meant he would have to visit the kitchens if he wanted any breakfast laid out this morning.

He found most of the servants gathered in this vast apartment, eagerly discussing the events that had disrupted their normal routine. William, the second footman, caught sight of him first. He sprang from his perch on the edge of the great working table and tugged his coat into a semblance of order. The excited voices silenced as the others scrambled to appear busy. One of the maids slipped out the door behind him.

Finley, his wooden expression giving him very much the appearance of a stuffed trout, stepped forward. "My lord—" he began, then didn't seem to know how to go on.

Daventry scanned the industriously working kitchen staff until his gaze fell on his cook. "Can you have something laid out for breakfast within the half hour? Thank you. Oh, and Colonel Marcome desires his valet to go to him." As he left, he could hear the mad scramble as everyone raced to their customary morning tasks.

He should have a few minutes to himself in which

he could go over the notes Mr. Charburton had made for him. Pleased, he headed for the estate office. He had barely taken a chair and started on the first page when a light tap sounded on the door, and William inched it ajar and stood uncertainly in the opening.

Daventry lowered the papers he held and regarded the man with a mixture of irritation and resignation. "Yes?"

The young man cleared his throat. "If you please, your lordship, Sir Joshua wishes to speak with you. He said he would be in the library."

With a sigh, Daventry made his way to that apartment, where he found Sir Joshua sprawled in a comfortable wing chair before the hearth, his feet propped on a stool and aimed at the blaze. "There you are," that gentleman said as Daventry entered. "Now, what's all this nonsense I've been hearing? Someone creeping about the house?"

Daventry drew his snuffbox from his pocket, but didn't open it. "We found no one."

Sir Joshua humphed. "Thought as much. Damn fool thing, to go scurrying about someone else's home. Stands to reason he'd only get himself caught. Heard my girl was hanging about helping."

Daventry stiffened. "She did not welcome my suggestion that she return to her room."

Her doting pappa snorted. "Shouldn't think she would. Well, if there was no one about, then there's no harm done. Planning on setting your fellows to keep guard every night?"

"Can you suggest an alternative?" He'd welcome one, and so, he'd wager, would his grooms.

"Get that Runner fellow to patrol the grounds. Long as he's here, might as well make himself useful. I want to see those rascally villains laid by the heels, though I doubt we'll recover much of what they took from the Court. Got Desdi's mamma's jewel box, you know."

Daventry looked up. "No, I hadn't known. I suppose that is why she's so determined to find them."

"Damn fool chit." Sir Joshua sighed. "Always been stubborn. Just like her mamma. Let's hope this Runner can do his job and bring them to book. I'll not rest easy until they're caught and my girl can't come to any harm."

At least he had an ally in his concerns for Desdi, Daventry reflected as he escorted Sir Joshua to the breakfast parlor at last. They found several of the others there before them, despite the earliness of the hour. Very few, it seemed, had returned to sleep after they had been disturbed.

As he settled at the table with a plate of rare beef and eggs, his glance strayed among his guests, noting Lady Eugenia's disgruntled expression, Bertie Cumberland's inability to keep his eyes open, Fanny Marcome's snappish temper.

Only Lady Xanthe and Miss Lynton appeared unruffled. Desdi's aunt sat beside his fairy godmother discussing the plans for the evening's entertainment. Words such as skits, scenery, costumes, and musical accompaniment drifted his way, reminding him that tonight they must present the scenes they had practiced.

Or not practiced enough, as the case might be.

He really ought to find Desdi and go over it once more. He glanced about the table again, realizing he had not set eyes upon the dratted girl for some time. When, precisely, had he last seen her? He racked his memory for any glimpse of her while he was searching the upper corridors, but drew a blank. He backtracked farther, to confronting her in the west wing, when he had clambered over the windowsill to join her. They had discussed the search and he had set forth to raise the alarm. He had assumed she'd follow.

She must have. Mustn't she?

Uneasiness stirred within him. She'd wanted to set forth after the miscreants upon the instant. But she'd listened to reason about waiting for Mr. Pimm to arrive, hadn't she?

Hadn't she?

He rose abruptly and made his way around the table until he stood between Xanthe and Charlotte Lynton. He leaned down, speaking softly for their ears alone. "Have you seen your niece this morning, Miss Lynton?"

Charlotte looked up quickly, her eyes widening. "She was not in her room. I assumed she had come down earlier, at the beginning of the commotion."

Cold seeped through him, but he forced an unconcerned smile to his lips. "Then she is undoubtedly back in the west wing, trying to see some clue we missed. I'll go fetch her." He gave her aunt a casual nod, as if not the least worry troubled him, and exited the apartment.

Not for a moment did he think she lingered in

the empty west wing. She'd exhausted its possibilities long ago. He could think of only one thing she would be likely to do, and his alarm grew. She'd follow the tracks, of course. But would she find anything—or anyone? He could only hope not. But she wouldn't give up, not his irritating, meddling, adventurous Desdi. Once she caught wind of a scent, no matter how faint, she'd pursue it with dogged determination.

They'd already sent for Mr. Pimm—hours ago, in fact. What the devil kept the man? He should have been here long ago. Daventry strode into the library and glanced at the clock, only to discover it lacked but ten minutes before nine. If the Runner had already been about the neighborhood when the groom reached the inn where he put up, it might take some time to track him down.

Time. He might have very little of that. Certainly none to waste with Desdi out and about and up to who knew what. He had best go after her. It shouldn't be that difficult to follow her tracks.

He let himself out the French doors leading onto the tiled terrace, descended the five shallow steps to the gravel path before the formal rose garden, and set off around the side of the house for the west wing. He had passed the stable and neared the track for the home farm when a gasping shout sounded behind him, and he turned to see Hewlett, his head groom, pelting along the path, waving his arm. Daventry waited as the man caught up, but it was a full minute before the little man could catch his breath.

"M'lord," Hewlett gasped at last, his chest still heaving. He held out a piece of paper.

Daventry unfolded it, glanced at the neatly printed message, and swore. His gaze fell on Hewlett, who eyed him with no little concern. "Did you read this?" he demanded.

The groom nodded. "Seeing as it weren't addressed to no one." He held out something gold.

With a sinking heart, Daventry recognized Desdi's locket. His hand clenched on it, and a vision of its hanging about her neck filled his mind. It had rested just below the hollow of her throat.

Hewlett sniffed. "Why'd they want to go and take a poor little innocent like 'er?"

"For ten thousand pounds." Daventry clenched his fist, crumpling the note. He forced himself to smooth it out and read it again. The money was to be left in a sack stuffed under the roots of the old gnarled oak behind the gate into the rectory's stable yard before noon if they wished the mort as wore the locket returned to them safe and sound. If they tried to find her, it went on, she would be killed. At once.

He couldn't think about that, what they might do to her—what they might already have done. He looked at the note again. "Where did you find this? Did you see anyone?"

"No." Hewlett's disgust sounded in his voice. "No one saw nothing. It were just sitting there, in the middle of the yard, when we come back from hunting 'bout the 'ouse."

On his own orders, Daventry reflected. He'd given

them the perfect opportunity to deliver their demand without being seen. But cursing himself for his lack of foresight would do nothing to bring Desdi back safe.

The note twitched in his unsteady fingers. He couldn't sit still, do nothing, simply wait. He'd go mad. And how could he trust in their promise not to harm her if the ransom was paid? They might well kill her anyway.

But he must appear to be complying with the demands, in case anyone kept an eye on him. He started back to the house. He would have to tell Sir Joshua, of course, and Miss Lynton. And Xanthe—

Xanthe. He wanted to see Xanthe. Now. If anyone could save Desdi, it would be she.

He retraced his route across the gravel, mounted the terrace steps, and within moments let himself back into the library. His mind shouted for the fairy to come to him, and as his eyes accustomed themselves to the interior darkness of the room, he could see her shimmering form.

"Where is she?" he demanded.

The fairy shook her head. "I cannot provide answers. I would if it were possible." She closed her eyes, humming softly, then shook her head.

"Can you keep her safe?" he demanded.

Xanthe clasped her hands. "I can only send out suggestions. Whether or not they are strong enough to prevail against a determined mind, I cannot know."

Opportunities only, he remembered with a touch

of bleakness. He had to solve his own problems. Right now, that meant finding ten thousand pounds.

He flung himself into a chair, staring at the hearth, his mind racing. There were a few hundreds locked in his desk drawer, meant to be presents for the staff and tenants. That didn't come anywhere close enough to the sum demanded. There were the rubies, secure in the vault, yet they were too well known for anyone but their rightful owner to dispose of them easily. And the men had specifically demanded flimsies.

"Xanthe?" He turned to see the fairy seated cross-legged in the air, a silver bowl hovering before her. "Can you conjure the sum they demanded?"

Xanthe actually smiled, and a moment later the soft strains of her humming reached him. They broke off abruptly. On the floor at his feet lay a sack, which opened to reveal neatly secured stacks of twenty pound notes.

"Thank you," he said, and knew it to be inadequate.

Xanthe settled to the floor, her expression somber. "Sir Joshua is on his way. I thought you would rather see him in here, alone."

He nodded. "You will do what you can for her?"

Xanthe laid a gentle hand on his shoulder. "We will, both Titus and I. I could only wish it were night," she added, mostly to herself.

"Night?"

A wry smile tugged at the corner of her mouth. "Starlight. You made your original wish while looking at the stars. Their presence now would strengthen any magic I do on your behalf."

He shook his head. "I don't believe I could bear it if she were still in their hands by nightfall."

Her steady violet gaze rested on him. "So you have finally come to recognize the desires of your heart?"

He nodded. "And God grant it may not be too late."

The door latch clicked behind him, and Xanthe glanced at it. "Here is Sir Joshua. I will leave you to tell him." She blew Daventry a kiss, hummed a rapid bar, and dissolved into a whirlwind of tiny colored particles that swirled upward to the ceiling and vanished. One lone feather drifted back to the carpet, rounded, almost translucent, its tip flecked with gold.

He picked it up, clutching it like a talisman. If only Desdi might have something to hold on to, something to give her some shred of hope, to sustain her.

"There you are, Daventry." Sir Joshua strode into the room. "Have you found my girl?"

Daventry turned. Something of his emotions must have shown in his face, for Sir Joshua stopped in his tracks, his jaw tightening, deep creases forming about his eyes. "What is it? What's happened to her?"

Daventry's glance fell on his desk, where the note lay open. Sir Joshua went to it, picked the paper up, and studied it. His fingers tightened on the sheet, and the blood drained slowly from his face.

"My God," he breathed at last. "Desdi? They've got my little girl? How?"

Daventry told him what he feared must have happened, and Sir Joshua sank onto the nearest chair. He leaned forward, his elbows on his knees, his head in his hands. After a long moment, he said, his voice trembling, "Confound the wretched brat. If only she weren't so stubborn and determined—" He broke off and drew a long, ragged breath. After a moment, he looked up. "What are we going to do? I don't know how I am to find so much money. How can they think it possible—"

"It's here." Daventry gestured toward the sack, which lay on the corner of the desk. "I—I've been gathering it."

Sir Joshua nodded. "Don't think I can thank you enough."

"There's no need." Daventry paced to the hearth, where he gripped the mantelpiece. "I never should have left her. I knew what she wanted to do. But I thought she'd enjoy searching the house—" He broke off, fighting back the emotion.

"She takes queer starts, my girl. No holding her back once she gets the bit between her teeth." Sir Joshua lowered his gaze to where his hands trembled in his lap. He looked old, shaken. After a moment, he looked up again. "What do we do now?"

Daventry studied the older man, noting the lines of strain, of despair. Abruptly, he said, "I had thought to have Mr. Pimm deliver the money. Would you care to accompany him?"

"Yes." Sir Joshua straightened. "Will you go, too?"

Daventry hesitated. "No. I intend to go after her at once."

Sir Joshua's eyes narrowed. "They said not to." He tapped the note.

Daventry drew a steadying breath. "Would you count on such men to keep their word about returning her safe if we comply?"

Sir Joshua hesitated, his expression flickering from hope to resignation to despair. "No."

"I intend to find her," Daventry informed him.

Sir Joshua studied his face, but said nothing.

"Don't worry. I'll bring her back safe. And then I will wring her lovely neck." On that savage note, he strode out the door.

Why the devil did he have to realize now, when he might have lost her, how very much he loved her, that his life would be empty and meaningless without her?

He went first to the gun room, where he took out the pistol he had carried through so many campaigns. He hefted it in his hand for a moment, remembering the weight and feel of it, then opened the drawer where he had stored the powder and shot. It took only moments to load the weapon. With it tucked safely in his waistband, he set forth once more for the west wing and the window with that damnable loose catch.

Here, though, he encountered his first setback. Sunlight now flooded the side of the house, and the shrubbery bed and snowy path that had offered such clear prints had turned to an unreadable muddy slush.

Still, he reminded himself, he didn't need to see for himself Desdi's small slippered prints. He knew those men had her. He had only to find them.

Fighting down his fear for her, he set forth along the path they had taken the other day, following traces of what might—or might not—have been the recent passage of many feet. No, they had to be recent. He wouldn't consider any other possibility. He *would* find Desdi.

At the footbridge he found the trace of a tiny print. Yesterday's—or this morning's? Hope surged through him and he forged ahead, not allowing the indeterminate signs of passage to weigh on his spirits. Yesterday, they had followed a definite trail to the well-trodden path behind the rectory. He would go there now, as quickly as he could, and hope he could discern which way the men—and Desdi—had gone from there.

He ducked beneath a low hanging branch, pushed another from his path, and strode through the clinging underbrush. At last he emerged into the small clearing beside the ancient oak, the oak where, in about two hours, Sir Joshua and Mr. Pimm would bring the sack of money. Opposite lay the gate to the shrub-shrouded stable yard, to his right a hedgerow bordering a field. To the village—or to the farms?

He stooped, examining the confused churning of the muddy ground. Was that another tiny print heading toward the village? He strode along that path, but could find no other indication that Desdi might have passed this way. The unclear signs had probably confused her, too. Had she started this way, then turned back?

He retraced his steps, then spotted what looked like the point of a narrow-toed slipper approaching the gate to the rectory yard. Could she have gone there, perhaps spoken to Mr. Doncaster or Mr. Beardsley? Perhaps one of them had seen her, might know in which direction she had headed. He swung the gate open and entered the yard.

Traces of mud smeared the cobbled stones, marking the passage of several people. He saw no one, but that didn't surprise him. From within the barn a horse stamped, and a rough voice swore. That brought him up short. An invective of that sort might be common in any army encampment, but not in these sanctified surroundings.

Curious, he made his way to where the broad stable door stood slightly ajar. A scraping sound, as of something heavy being dragged across a stone floor, reached him. Alert, yet feeling a bit of a fool for his sudden uneasiness, he moved with stealth, positioning himself where he could just see into the dimly illuminated area.

A trunk lay in the center of the floor, its lid open. He could make out a cloth-wrapped shape protruding from the top. As he watched, a great-coated figure came into view, a rough man he didn't recognize, who shrouded something that gleamed within a torn piece of sheeting. He set this in the trunk, then disappeared back the way he had come. A few moments later he returned, this time carrying a three-branched candelabrum.

The housebreakers here? At the rectory? Then Desdi might—

A footstep scraping behind him brought him around, reaching for the pistol he had stowed in his waistband. His fingers closed over it, only to release it again as his gaze fell on one of Manton's exquisite dueling pieces, pointed directly at his chest.

Mr. Beardsley frowned at him. "I distinctly told you not to come looking for that meddling chit. Now I shall have to dispose of both of you, I suppose. You are causing me the devil of a lot of trouble."

"You have her." Daventry barely breathed the words.

"Of course I do. I couldn't very well leave her prowling about, any more than I can leave you."

"What have you done with her?" Daventry stepped forward, fury raging within him.

Mr. Beardsley drew back a pace, the point of his pistol wavering. Daventry thrust it aside with a swift blow, then sprang on the curate, carrying them both to the ground. One of his hands closed about Beardsley's throat, his sole intention to choke Desdi's whereabouts out of him, when the scrape of a nailed boot reminded him—too late—they were not alone. He spun into a crouch, half dragging the curate with him, then something collided with his head. For a moment sound pulsed in his ears and lights danced before his eyes; then all receded into silence and darkness as he pitched forward into unconsciousness.

Twelve

Noise reached him first, an infernal ringing in his ears. This faded after a moment, only to be replaced by a muffled scraping sounding somewhere in the distance. Then cold enveloped him, a dank chill that pervaded his bones. Figuring out the whats and wheres seemed too much trouble, so he lay still, convinced it would all sort itself out soon enough. It had the last time he'd been wounded.

Wounded. From long soldiering experience he checked his arms. He couldn't move them. His eyes shot open, and he winced at the light that bathed his face.

"Are you all right?" A soft voice, female. Desdi's.

He jerked his head around to find her, sending pain shooting through his temple. He winced, then tried to speak. It came forcibly home to him someone had gagged him. He blinked, clearing his blurred vision, and his gaze fell on her.

She knelt near him, her face close, her eyes sparkling, a rag knotted about her chin, her hands behind her. Hands. He wriggled his own and found them securely fastened behind his back. Someone had bound his ankles, too. Yet relief at finding her un-harmed, so very much herself, outweighed any con-cern.

"I have almost gotten your feet unfastened," she told him, her voice bright and disconcertingly cheer-ful. "If you will sit up, I will concentrate on your hands. You've been lying on them," she added.

What he wanted was to rid himself of this gag, to ask a few pertinent questions.

"Can you?" she prompted. "Sit up, I mean."

He could, though it wasn't easy with the waves of dizziness that washed over him. As soon as he caught his balance, she began a laborious crawling that brought her behind him. He managed to turn sideways, making it easier for her bound hands to reach his wrists. He could feel her fingers, their brushing touch, their tugging as she worked on the rope that secured him.

He'd found her. At the moment, that outweighed every other consideration. He'd found her safe and unharmed. At least he'd seen no mark of injury on her, and her spirits seemed remarkably ebullient. Now he had only to get her out of this mess before anyone came back for them.

He glanced about their stone-walled prison. Light filtered in through a pair of high, narrow windows, heavily begrimed and streaked with cobwebs. A bat-tered trunk and two wooden crates stood against one moisture-studded wall, with lengths of frayed rope lying in an untidy heap on top of one. He couldn't see anything else from this angle, only feel the chill dankness of the air.

Desdi continued her awkward labors in a silence that bespoke an intense concentration and considerable patience. It took time, possibly too much time. He twitched, a frustrated movement, earning a teasing rebuke from her. At least her humor remained unimpaired. His own temper was rapidly reaching a breaking point. What the devil was Xanthe about? he fumed. Or was this another of the "opportunities" she'd granted him?

"I cannot imagine why I never practiced knot untying behind my back," Desdi exclaimed after more precious minutes had raced past. "It is odd, is it not, how we never school ourselves in the skills that truly matter in life?"

It was a skill she never should have had any need to acquire, he fumed, silent against his will.

"And at the moment," she sighed, "it is the very one I need most."

She sounded so reasonable, so matter-of-fact, they might be discussing the merest commonplace rather than an attempt to save themselves—perhaps save their very lives. Did nothing ever send Desdi into a pucker?

He should be grateful, of course, that she didn't indulge in a fit of the vapors, yet her matter-of-fact attitude toward her capture and imprisonment denied him any chance to play the dashing rescuer. He'd envisioned saving her, comforting her, soothing her fears, while she looked up to him, her worshipful gaze acknowledging him her hero.

Some hero he made. He knelt here, helpless, while she made jokes and rescued *him*. On the whole, he decided with savage feeling, he wished he had never heard of fairy godmothers.

She let out a sigh of relief. "Here it comes."

Miraculously, he felt the ropes ease, then slip away. The next moment he'd brought his hands before him, rubbing them briskly, easing the chafing pain at his wrists. As soon as his fingers functioned properly, he unfastened the rope that bound his mouth and spat out the greasy, rancid-tasting rag that had gagged him.

"How long was I unconscious?" he demanded in a harsh, low tone.

"Twenty minutes, perhaps." She struggled around, presenting her own tightly fastened wrists to him.

What he needed was a knife. He checked his pocket but found no trace of the small one he always carried, nor of his watch. They had taken his pistol, as well. Anger surged through him, not at the cavalier treatment they had meted out to him, but at their taking the weapon that had accompanied him throughout the Peninsular campaign. He would get it back, even if it meant having to tear each of those villains apart piece by piece.

His gaze fell on Desdi's bent, disheveled head. He'd tear them apart anyway for what they had done to her.

He managed to free the knots tightened by her struggles. Then they both turned their attention to the ropes securing their ankles. At last he pulled his rope free. Desdi had almost finished her own, so he left her to it.

Now to get out. He crossed to the stair and laid

a hand on the railing. Solid, he noted with satisfaction. Still, he exercised considerable caution as he put his weight on the bottom step, then eased himself to the next. If anyone remained above, guarding them, he did not want to alert them with a betraying creak of old wood.

When he came within reach of the ceiling, he pushed against the ill-fitting square of wood that must be a trapdoor. It didn't budge. He tried again, harder, to no avail.

"Secured?" Desdi's voice sounded resigned.

"I fear so." He turned to see her standing on the other side of the room, her gaze now studying the windows set so high above her. From outside, he remembered, they rested about a foot above the ground level, their purpose undoubtedly to let light and air into this underground storage room.

"We'll have to stack a few of those crates," Desdi said after a moment's silence.

He returned to the cold stone floor and examined the wooden boxes. Three seemed too rickety for him to use, but two others felt solid—heavy, in fact, from whatever contents they held. He pushed against the largest, and the resulting grate set his teeth on edge. He shook his head. "The noise of shoving these under the window would bring them down here as fast as they could run."

Desdi wrinkled her nose. "Then we shall have to carry them."

He tested a corner and found the weight daunting. "If you were a man, we could do it with ease. But as you are not—"

"Oh, for heaven's sake," she snapped. "I am not helpless. And if we cannot move it," she added with all the air of delivering a clincher, "then I shall have to contrive to scramble onto your shoulders and stand there while I either open or break a window. Which is it to be? And do let us hurry. I have no desire to simply sit here and wait to be murdered."

He cast her a fulminating look and seized one end of the heaviest crate. She grasped the other, somewhat hesitantly in spite of her bravado, and tugged. Game as a pebble, he reflected, but sadly wanting in strength.

Taking as much weight as he could, he half lifted, half dragged the crate across the stone floor. Desdi, her face grim and determined, eased her end along, and somehow they kept the scraping noise to a minimum. At last he set it down beneath the window and gave himself a moment to rest.

Already, Desdi had started back for the next. This one, as he'd already determined, weighed less. He managed to carry it with very little help from her until he reached the first. Lifting the one he carried high enough to slide it onto the other proved no easy feat, but he accomplished it at last.

"Well done," breathed Desdi, eyeing him with approval. "Now, if you will lend me your hand, I will climb upon this one—" She suited action to words, then started to scramble onto the next crate.

She teetered, and he leaped to her side, grasping her about the waist. She swayed against him, and for one moment all thought of their predicament vanished from his mind. He was aware only of the

scent and feel of her, the rough material of her pelisse—no, she wore his greatcoat, and probably that
flimsy night dress beneath it.

"Give me your hand." She grabbed it to steady
herself.

Thus forcibly recalled to a sense of their incar-
ceration, he boosted her slight form onto the upper
crate, vividly aware of the slimness of her body, the
soft curves beneath the coarse material. "Careful,"
he said, but whether to her or himself, he wasn't
quite certain. He couldn't let himself be distracted—
not now, not yet. Later. The last he made a promise.

For a moment her hand rested on his shoulder.
Then she straightened, supporting herself on the
wall, until her fingers just brushed one of the long,
narrow panes. She changed her position, her hand
following the glass until she found a catch. "There,"
she breathed. The window gave a protesting creak
as she pushed the pane outward.

"Good girl." He eased himself onto the top crate
at her side. It shifted under his weight, but he
wouldn't be there long if he could help it. He caught
her foot as if he were to throw her into a saddle,
and in another moment she lay on her stomach, half
through the open window. She squirmed, kicking
slightly, awarding him an entrancing glimpse of a
pair of very well-turned ankles. Then she rolled,
pulling herself through.

Only a moment passed before her face reappeared. "Can you make it? Or shall I run around
and open the trapdoor?"

"And risk getting caught?" He grabbed the sill

with both hands and hefted himself up. By angling his body, he was able to duck his shoulders through the window, though his head collided with the glass with a resounding crack.

A sound that might have been either a gasp or a suppressed giggle escaped Desdi. She moved back, allowing him room to maneuver his legs through the inadequate opening. A minute later he pulled himself to his knees, aware of how very cold was the ground beneath him.

Desdi sat back on her heels, her eyes bright. "We made it!"

"This far, at least." He stood, then held down a hand to her.

She took it and came to her feet, retaining her hold, squeezing his fingers. "I think we did that rather well."

He could think of other things he'd like to try with her, but all involved being somewhere safe and undisturbed—which meant they had to get out of the rectory yard before those men appeared again, and that might well be soon, for they would want to collect the ransom for Desdi.

He started to reach for his watch, remembered it had been taken from him, and bit back an oath. The sun neared its zenith, which meant it must be nearing noon. Mr. Pimm and Desdi's father might soon be here bearing the bag of money, and Mr. Pimm would probably have a gun.

And that reminded him, he intended to retrieve his favorite pistol.

He glanced at Desdi and caught the gleam in her

bright green eyes. If he didn't plan their course of action quickly, she might do so herself, with who knew what disastrous results.

They could always wait here and hope they weren't discovered, but he didn't see that course of nonaction appealing to her. It didn't appeal to him, either. They might as easily be recaptured as rescued.

The best chance would be to take the risk, to slip across the yard and out the gate, then try to reach Mr. Pimm and have him send for his patrol before the villains realized what had occurred. Once those men discovered he and Desdi no longer languished in their prison, they might well cut their losses and run. He did not want them to escape.

Desdi's fingers tightened on his. "What are we waiting for?" she hissed. She started forward, still clinging to him, moving with unexpected caution.

He liked the feel of her hand secure in his. He'd like it even more if he led. Positioning himself before her, he moved to the edge of the building and peered into the cobbled yard. No one. But that provided only partial reassurance.

About twenty yards separated them from the gate, but it was open, unsheltered space, offering no hope of concealment. Once away from the wall against which they crouched, they would be vulnerable, easily spotted and easily recaptured. The risk bothered him not at all, but he had Desdi to consider.

Her grip tightened on his hand. "Ready?" The word came out on a whisper.

She made her own decisions, he realized. That

knowledge both shook and pleased him. He didn't risk her; she risked herself. With the security of her fingers clasped tight in his own, he took a step forward.

The sound of a door creaking reached him. Desdi drew back, pulling him with her. Daventry strained his hearing as gravel crunched beneath more than one pair of feet.

"My dear Mr. Doncaster," came Mr. Beardsley's voice. "You have given the same Christmas sermon for several years now, or so I have been told. There is not the least need to practice it."

"But I have made changes," came the old man's plaintive tones. "Really, my dear Mr. Beardsley, I should be so very grateful if you would hear it once more."

"I've already heard it three times this morning," came the short answer. "And now I fear there are matters I must tend to."

The crunching had grown gradually louder. That the curate, at least, intended to enter the stable yard seemed certain. Daventry gestured for Desdi to remain where she was, then ducked across the scant five yards that separated the side of the stable from the shrubbery that lined the garden wall of the rectory. He drew as far into this as he could penetrate, waiting, his heart pounding, his spirits soaring at being able to take some definite action at last. If Beardsley came out alone, he would take him down before the man had a chance to cry out. If the rector came with him—well, that would make matters a trifle more complicated, but not impossible.

The hinges on the garden gate squeaked, and Mr. Doncaster tottered into the yard, Beardsley at his heels. "Why do you not go back to your study?" the curate suggested, maneuvering in front of the elderly man and blocking his way. "I must just check on the cob, for he seemed a trifle stiff in the knee yesterday. Then I will return and we may go through the sermon once more."

Mr. Doncaster patted him on the shoulder. "Such a fine morning. The little walk will do me good, and you may tell me if you think that part about love conquering all should be stressed a little more." He moved to pass his curate. "I most particularly wish people to remember it."

Beardsley moved to block him once more, placing himself where he stared in Daventry's direction. The earl drew back into the shrubs, cursing his ill luck, and the faintest crackle sounded as a branch broke. Beardsley looked up, straight at Daventry, and shock registered clearly in his face. The man let out a shout, and Daventry threw caution to the winds and charged him. The curate grabbed the startled rector, keeping him before him, preventing Daventry from attacking.

Two of the ruffians emerged from the stable. They stopped, staring at Daventry, their expressions incredulous. "What's 'e doing loose?" demanded one.

The other, displaying a more practical nature, ducked back into the stable, only to emerge the next moment with a stout stick and a pitchfork. The latter he handed to his companion, then started forward, hefting his cudgel in his hands as if gauging its weight and ability to do serious damage to an opponent.

Daventry hesitated, watching the two men advancing on him, seeing the utterly perplexed and horrified expression on the poor rector's face, noting the grim set of Beardsley's mouth. Somewhere just out of his sight stood Desdi, undoubtedly making untenable and dangerous plans of her own to extricate them from this predicament. If only he had a weapon—any weapon.

He caught a blur of movement; then Beardsley gave a sharp cry and grasped his upper arm. Another stone followed the first, this one missing him. A third sailed with more accuracy, striking him in the chest.

"Over there!" shouted the curate, gesturing to where Desdi peeped out from behind the stable, another rock already in her hand.

The man with the pitchfork charged her, and Daventry threw himself after the man, tackling him before he'd gone more than six paces. They landed on the cobbled stones, rolling, struggling.

Someone shouted, "Don't move."

Irrationally, Daventry thought it sounded like Frederick. But whoever it was, Daventry ignored the warning, instead grappling with Desdi's would-be assailant. The explosion of a pistol rent the air, but not until he had planted his man a facer, laying him out cold on the cobbled stones, did he look up.

The shout sounded again, and he glanced behind him to see his cousin Frederick storming across the yard, a pistol gripped awkwardly in his left hand.

Charlotte Lynton ran along the path just beyond the forest hedge, only stopping as she reached the open gate. She clutched the post, her eyes wide with horror.

Beardsley released the rector and lunged at Frederick, bearing down on his one arm, struggling, trying to wrest the gun from his determined grasp. As Daventry lurched to his feet, Charlotte Lynton screamed, then a stunning blow struck Daventry across the shoulders. He fell to one knee, then lunged into the man's next attack as the cudgel swung at him once more. The man fell back, the wind knocked out of him, but before Daventry could claim the branch he had wielded, his first opponent, who had regained his senses, charged toward him, only to trip neatly over the handle of the pitchfork thrust between his legs by Desdi. The man sprawled forward, and Daventry swung the recovered cudgel to good effect.

He spun to where Frederick and Beardsley still fought for the pistol. Reaching them in two running strides, he grasped the curate by the collar, hauled him from his cousin, and planted him a leveler. Frederick sat up as Charlotte flung herself to the ground beside him, embracing him, tears streaming down her cheeks. His one arm went about her and shakily he stroked her hair, murmuring in a soothing tone.

"Was that what is known as 'darkening his daylights' and 'drawing his cork?' " Desdi, her gaze resting on the prostrate curate, sounded somewhat shaky but lively as ever.

The earl grinned. "Only among the vulgar. You should not use boxing cant, you know."

She ignored this, regarding instead the spectacle of Captain Frederick Grayson kissing her prim and proper Aunt Charlotte.

"What the devil's going on here?" demanded a new voice, and Sir Joshua strode up, the sack of money clutched loosely in his hand. Mr. Pimm followed at his heels, dragging along another of the ruffians, whose hands remained bound behind his back. Sir Joshua strode into the yard, acknowledged Desdi's safety with a short nod, then turned to his sister. "Explain yourself, Charlotte."

Charlotte Lynton started to pull free from Frederick's embrace, but the disobliging captain held her close. For a long moment Frederick looked into her eyes, an expression of awed wonder in his own; then he transferred his gaze to Sir Joshua. "I believe, sir, I am about to have the honor of becoming your brother-in-law."

Sir Joshua straightened. "Damme if I can't make you out, Charlotte. Here I've thought you were mooning about the place over Daventry, and hard put to it I've been to know what to say once it became clear as a pikestaff you wouldn't suit. And now I find you've been playing a deep game all along." He shook his head. "Well, I wish you happy, my dear." He bent to shake Frederick's left hand. "You'll not regret your choice, Grayson. Devilish fine girl, m'sister.

"I know." Frederick turned back to Charlotte and brushed a lingering tear from her cheek with his fingertip. "Devilish fine," he murmured, making the words an endearment and a caress.

Daventry looked away, to Desdi at his side. The ridiculous chit grinned openly, her face lively and glowing, as if she had not been subjected to rough treatment, imprisoned in a cellar, and taken part in a rough and tumble fight. She'd enjoyed it, in fact.

And so, he realized, had he. Inheriting the title and responsibilities had not completely buried his sense of adventure—which was just as well, considering what he was about to do.

A groan from the ground recalled his attention, and he turned to assist Mr. Pimm and Sir Joshua in securing their prisoners. This took some considerable time, during which Charlotte and Frederick escorted the rector, still badly shaken, to his house.

The prisoners secured, Mr. Pimm appropriated Mr. Beardsley's cob and rode to fetch the men he had left guarding the various roads and paths. Daventry, leaving Sir Joshua to keep watch, followed Pimm out into the yard and saw him off.

He returned to find Desdi in the stable, pulling the sheet-wrapped contents from one of the trunks. He regarded her with amused exasperation, for she seemed oblivious to his presence. She continued her inspection for several more minutes, then without glancing at him, said, "Are you not going to help?"

He strolled forward. "Let me guess. Your mamma's jewelry box?"

"Well, of course." She unwrapped a small chest, revealing a corner, and set it aside. "It could be anywhere, I fear."

"It will turn up when the authorities go through all these things." He took a bulky epergne from her hands, replaced it in the trunk, and led her out into the pale wintry sunlight.

Desdi sank onto the bench that ran along the garden wall, and smiled up at him, mischief glinting in her lovely eyes. He gazed at her, his mind racing. He felt alive, invigorated, as if he had carried off a successful maneuver.

A new and startling realization struck him. He'd thought the order and discipline of the military had appealed to him, but it had been the hurdles and obstacles, the unexpectedness, the games of cat and mouse they had played with the enemy, that he had loved. He thrived on challenge.

Xanthe had known it all along. Lord, he'd been a fool. She'd granted him an opportunity, all right: this whole ordeal. He could almost hear the fairy's voice warning him not to let his chance for happiness rather than orderliness slip through his fingers.

But was he too late? Could Desdi love him, in spite of all he had said, all he had been? He knew of only one way to find out.

He settled on the bench at her side. She looked up at him, her expression speculative, but made no move to slide over to give him more room. That suited him perfectly.

After a moment, she turned to stare straight ahead. "I am very sorry Aunt Charlotte has chosen your cousin instead of you. I thought—"

"Your father was quite right. We should not have

suited, and it has never been your aunt I have wanted to marry."

She cast him a dubious look.

Logic and quiet protestations would get him nowhere with Desdi. Throwing caution to the winds, he dragged her into his arms. A startled exclamation escaped her. Then his mouth claimed hers, and he kissed her with all the desire he had tried so hard to repress.

When at last he let her breathe, she stared at him, eyes wide. Abruptly she flung her arms about his neck and dragged his head down so she could kiss him again. When she could speak, she said, "My tendency to treat everything as a rare joke will probably drive you to Bedlam."

Soberly, but with his eyes twinkling, he said, "Very true. But it will be an enjoyable journey."

She tilted her head to one side. "We had best hire a very capable housekeeper, one who is not given to drink."

"I will give that top priority."

She frowned. "I can probably launch Bella into society, and I do know how to go on, truly I do, only—"

"Only it might be wiser to entrust that task to your aunt Charlotte?" he inquired.

Desdi turned slightly in the circle of his arms to fix him with a serious gaze. "Bella will behave just as she ought, I feel certain. But Sophie is another matter. I fear she will regard my own levity as a *carte blanche* to behave in any outrageous manner she chooses."

"Very likely," he agreed. "Definitely, we shall speak to your aunt. Have you any other objections to our marriage?"

She frowned, obviously subjecting the matter to no little consideration. At last, she said, "Not at present. But if you will give me time—"

"Absolutely not," he declared. "I am tempted to get a special license rather than posting the banns, if such speed is necessary."

She brightened. "Do you know, a flight to Gretna Green might be the most capital fun. Only consider, it seems fraught with potential for the most diverting larks."

"You should not like it at all," he assured her. "Besides, I have an ambition to see how much chaos you can create out of a simple church wedding."

A gleam lit her eyes, and hastily he gathered her once more into his arms, distracting her in the most delightful manner possible.

Epilogue

Xanthe hummed softly and passed a hand across the water that filled the chased silver bowl. In the mirrored interior, she could still see Desdi and Daventry locked in one another's arms, oblivious to all else. She smiled and allowed the surface to ripple, as if stirred by a breeze.

The image fractured, breaking into myriad sparkling facets, and the water roiled and bubbled. Xanthe hummed another note, and the restless waters stilled. A single star glowed in the depths, burning a brilliant ice blue. It flickered, other stars appeared about it, and then they all faded. Only sunlight reflected in the shallow depths, dappled with the pattern of the lace curtains that hung in the window of her bedchamber.

Titus, who sat on the dresser top peering into the bowl, let out a short *myap*.

Xanthe smiled, somewhat mistily, at the now clear waters. "No, he doesn't need our magic anymore. He has found his own."

A series of staccato sounds escaped the cat.

The fairy godmother looked up, affronted. "Well,

how could I tell him she was in no danger at those men's hands? He wouldn't have realized how much he loved her if I had. Some men are so stubborn they have to be shocked out of themselves."

The tip of the full white tail twitched.

"Oh, you need have no fears on that score. They will be wonderfully happy, never doubt it. All three of her sons will take after her and be forever in some scrape or other. He will be so proud of them all it will never cross his mind he never has a moment's peace."

One of the cat's ears twitched, and he opened his mouth in a silent meow.

Xanthe smiled. "Of course they find her mamma's jewelry box. It was in the crate she stood on when they climbed through that cellar window. Dear child. If she had known, I daresay she would have refused to escape until she had it safe once more."

Titus half closed his eyes.

"The pistol? Oh, Aubrey's, you mean. Yes, they will find that later this afternoon in Mr. Beardsley's bedchamber. All will be settled most satisfactorily. Most satisfactorily, indeed."

A rumble sounded in the cat's throat.

Xanthe stared at him. "Good heavens, I was quite forgetting. Thank you, my dear. A housekeeper. A very capable housekeeper. I shall find them one for a wedding present."

The cat blinked his gleaming eyes.

"Of course we shall stay. I do enjoy weddings. And this one will be quite out of the common way—you may be sure of that. Can you truly imagine anything involving Desdi proceeding with decorous normality? What with the poor dear rector losing his place in the service, and the doves I shall summon into the church, I believe we shall have quite the most delightful time."

Titus's tail twitched again.

Xanthe shook her head. "Not immediately, no. I believe we may enjoy a short respite before our next summons. What?" she added at the cat's imperious stare. "I'm not sure."

She picked up a candle that lay beside the bowl, then set it back. No, not candles. Her fingers touched the star-shaped holder in which the taper stood. No, not stars, either. She turned to the window and gazed up into the early afternoon sky. Sunlight? No, that didn't feel right, either. Not this time.

She rested her elbows on the sill, her thoughts drifting with the breeze. A waxing three-quarter moon rose in the sky, hovering just above the line of yew trees.

A moon . . . her mischievous smile flashed. Moonlight it would be. She turned back into the room, ready to enjoy whatever came next.

BOOK YOUR PLACE ON OUR WEBSITE AND MAKE THE READING CONNECTION!

We've created a customized website just for our very special readers, where you can get the inside scoop on everything that's going on with Zebra, Pinnacle and Kensington books.

When you come online, you'll have the exciting opportunity to:

- View covers of upcoming books
- Read sample chapters
- Learn about our future publishing schedule (listed by publication month *and author*)
- Find out when your favorite authors will be visiting a city near you
- Search for and order backlist books from our online catalog
- Check out author bios and background information
- Send e-mail to your favorite authors
- Meet the Kensington staff online
- Join us in weekly chats with authors, readers and other guests
- Get writing guidelines
- AND MUCH MORE!

**Visit our website at
http://www.zebrabooks.com**

A MAGICAL MOMENT

Damn Xanthe, Daventry swore inwardly. Her magic worked at the wrong moment, when he danced with the wrong lady. And why must they wear gloves? He would much rather be holding her hand without the supple leather between them. He certainly didn't want to release her as required by the movement, but he did, and forced himself to look straight ahead as she circled him once more, rather than allowing his gaze to follow her every light step, her every provocative, swaying movement. Her curls bounced—not much, just enough to make him aware of them, of her.

She wasn't the right lady to be his wife. His militarily pragmatic side knew this, set off claxons and alarums in his mind, warned him he must not indulge this dangerous whim. He could do nothing that might raise her expectations. He could not, must not, offer for her. He needed a practical, sensible wife, not some giddy child who would sweep him off into larks and games. He needed a helpmate to be lady of the manor, to carry soup to ailing tenants, to assist the rector with his concerns in the parish. He needed a worldly wise chaperon to guide his sisters through the pitfalls of their coming London Seasons. Yet with every passing moment, it became harder to heed such practical counsel.

He wanted Desdemona, and a long-buried reckless streak stirred within him, whispering to let practical matters be damned.

Books by Janice Bennett

REGENCIES

AN ELIGIBLE BRIDE
TANGLED WEB
MIDNIGHT MASQUE
AN INTRIGUING DESIRE
A TEMPTING MISS
A LADY'S CHAMPION
THE MATCHMAKING GHOST
THE CANDLELIGHT WISH

REGENCY MYSTERIES

A MYSTERIOUS MISS
A DANGEROUS INTRIGUE
A DESPERATE GAMBLE

TIME TRAVELS

A TIMELY AFFAIR
FOREVER IN TIME
A CHRISTMAS KEEPSAKE
A TOUCH OF FOREVER
ACROSS FOREVER

FUTURISTIC

AMETHYST MOON

Published by Zebra Books and Pinnacle